KINKY WOLF

AN ALPHA WOLVES LOVE CURVES NOVEL

AIDY AWARD

Cover by Jaqueline Sweet

THE FATE OF WOLFKIND IS IN HIS BROKEN HANDS~

Niko Troika gave up everything, his pack, his best friend, his ability to shift, to ensure the entire wolf-shifter society wasn't exposed. He saved them all from total destruction, but he simply doesn't have anything left to save himself. Under the light of a full moon, he finds his salvation...in her. His one true mate. The one woman whose heart he broke and would never love him again.

Zara's been to hell, and it's filled with greedy wolf-shifters. She won't let anything stop her from her crusade to save anyone else from being driven insane like she was. Not even love.

But the two of them are caught in the middle of a pack war, and something dark and sinister doesn't want either of them to remember who or what they truly are.

If you live among wolves,
you have to howl like a wolf

— RUSSIAN PROVERB

CURSED

*N*iko lay sweaty and naked under the full moon. He stared up at the goddess who'd done this to him and cursed her name.

He'd chosen to sacrifice everything to her. Keeping her and all of wolfkind safe were worthy causes. He should have been rewarded with an afterlife of fluffy clouds and mountains of bacon. Instead he had a broken mind and his ability to shift into his wolf...gone.

What was he supposed to do now?

Stop fucking feeling sorry for himself, for a start. So, he wasn't a wolf shifter. He wasn't an Alpha anymore either and would never lead his own pack into the future. So what if he'd given up everything good in his life, including his true mate?

His brothers were safe, mated to their true mates, and each had their own packs now. The Volkovs weren't going to pull wolfkind back into the dark ages, and that should be enough.

He'd done more than his duty. Pride in that should sustain him for a thousand years.

Niko's heart beat hard against his chest and his vision

tunneled. Doc had said if the darkness swirled, he could just say he would think about it tomorrow and then find something else to focus on. Like he was some kind of spoiled Southern belle.

Nothing could steal his mind away when the plague of despair infected him. Killing his best friend wasn't exactly the kind of trauma he'd simply get over. That night haunted him, hunted him, horrified him.

He wouldn't think about that now. He wouldn't think about the Volkovs, Russia, or the tragedy he'd caused right now. He'd think about that tomorrow.

Only one other memory he could call on pushed away the attack of anguish threatening to drown him. He'd retreated into the gentle caress of this oblivion too often, using the warmth he found there like a drug. She was his crutch, a way to numb everything else. He wasn't ready for rehab.

Niko closed his eyes on the night, ignoring the pull of the full moon, for the brilliant beautiful glow of Zara. He let the bright light of the memory take over his mind. The tension in his muscles melted away, the specters of self-hatred receded, all replaced by her.

If only they were both still teenagers. If only he hadn't broken up with her when he left for Russia. He wouldn't think about that now.

His vision of her wasn't fuzzy or marred with age. She was as clear and crisp as 8K television just like she was every time he thought of her. She smiled at him, and he reached for her, needing so much to bask in her sweetness.

Only this time, her smile faltered, a flash of hurt and sorrow crossed her face, and tears flowed from her eyes. Niko reached to wipe them away. When he touched their wetness, his fingers were on his own face.

Zara wasn't the one crying. He was. Fuck. Not again.

Instead of reliving his favorite memory of their first night together so long ago, he was back at the battle for Kosta's pack. Back to lying on the ground, bleeding, waiting for Zara to recognize him. Seeing her held captive by that asshole, Ramsey Crescent, had nearly ripped his soul from his body. Especially knowing he couldn't do anything to help her.

He was helpless. So weak, so disconnected from everything he'd ever known... So alone.

Niko opened his eyes and filled his vision with the bright light of the moon. Even she had forsaken him. The pull of her magic, the urge to shift into his wolf, pulled on him from deep inside. When he sought out the beast within, it didn't answer.

Niko didn't deserve to have the wolf any longer. Not since he'd abused his Alpha strength and power. Not since Russia. The depths of his misdeeds roiled in his chest and stomach, and he quickly rolled in the grass, hurling bile and acid into the leaves.

He stayed hunched over, dry heaving and gasping for air until, finally, the nausea subsided. It took a few more minutes for the ringing in his head and the cold sweat to recede. He deserved every second of his miserable existence, but he was damn tired of it.

Either he stopped wallowing in this stagnant and deadly misery, or he fucking did something about changing the destructive path he was on. Being the alpha of the Troikas was off the table. Without his wolf, pretty much anything he'd ever imagined for his own future was no longer an option.

Fine. But he wouldn't be a drain on his family. He could

still be a productive member of the pack. His life would be that of a mere mortal now. Humans did lots of things wolves could do, too. Some of his best friends were humans.

Someone he loved was human.

Maybe, just maybe, if he could prove himself worthy, and make himself into a better man than he'd ever been a wolf, he could win her back.

That was probably too much to ask.

He would try anyway. He had to. At this point, it was either pull his head out of his ass, or wallow in the darkness surrounding him until he died. Real happiness may not be in the cards for him ever again, not with a vital part of himself missing, but winning Zara's heart back and seeing her happy might be as close as he could get.

A lump formed in his throat, and he had to swallow down the fear that he could pull the beautiful angel down into his own hell. He would have to guard her from his darkness, not let her see his true self cowering in the hidden places of his mind. Niko would protect her

If she would have him. That was no guarantee. It was a place to start, though.

In slow, measured movements, he got to his feet. One vertebra at a time, he stood up straight. The light of the moon was brighter now, neither clouds, nor Niko's own dark thoughts blocked the rays calling to his blood. He'd spent his last night as a wolf in her glow, so it was right that he took his final night before embracing a new human life to bask under her as well.

Tomorrow, in the sunshine, the full moon would be no more than it was to any other human. No, her light would now symbolize his rebirth as an ordinary, average Joe Schmoe. A Joe who had wrongs of the past to right.

Starting with the woman whose heart he broke.

If he had his wolf, he'd sneak over to the hospital where Zara healed from the wounds, both mental and physical, inflicted on her by those damn Bay Pack wolves. He would watch over her in her sleep and make sure no shifter ever bothered her again.

Think like a human, stupid. Humans didn't watch each other sleep unless they were creepy stalkers. That meant he would wait until a reasonable hour in the morning and go see her during normal hospital visiting hours.

He'd bring her flowers... ugh, bouquets were nothing more than dead plants. Fine then, a small flowering plant in a pot. His mother should know where he could get something like that in town. Niko had been in Russia for so long, he hardly knew his way around his own hometown anymore.

Sleepy Folk, the speakeasy bar his family owned, was still going strong, especially since Max had taken over the day-to-day operations. Maybe Niko could help out there. He was part owner. The bar was a safer choice than Kosta's club.

That place reminded him a little too much of the clubs he and Mik spent time in during the long, cold Russian winters. Although, The Naughty Wolf was a hell of a lot tamer than the BDSM clubs owned by the Volkovs.

Niko picked up his pace and jogged through the Reserve and back toward the pack house. No way he should be thinking about domination and submission and Zara in the same thought.

He broke into a run.

No way he should be thinking of Zara on her knees,

wrapped in miles of red rope, her thighs spread, her pussy dripping wet for him.

Niko sprinted through the trees, letting the bushes scrape his legs and the branches slap his face, neck, and arms.

No way in hell should he even entertain the thought of having her across his lap, her plump soft ass in the air, pink from his spankings, begging him to let her come.

The muscles in his body burned, his lungs matching the pain as Niko pushed himself to run beyond the bounds of his humanly form. Faster, harder, he had to push his body so he could stop thinking about hers and all the things he wanted to do to it. The forested area of the Reserve opened into his family's spacious backyard, and Niko gave one final burst of speed.

Wolves howled not far off, probably scenting his desperation. Max and Kosta patrolled their expanded territories along with their Enforcers. There wasn't much the patrols missed, and there was likely already rounds of gossip spreading through the ranks about him.

That was nothing new. Being the heir to one of the most powerful packs around had given Niko plenty of practice being in the spotlight of wolf culture. He'd been destined to be a star. How he had fallen.

All he wanted now was to fade into obscurity. Let everyone forget he'd been groomed to be the best of the best alphas. Because then maybe they also wouldn't remember he was the right-hand man of the Wolf Tzar, whose death had thrown their entire world into chaos.

Whose death was all his fault.

The one person who didn't give a shit was Zara. She hadn't even known about werewolves like him until recently. She'd probably be happy he wasn't a wolf anymore. One more reason he had to find a way to win her back.

Niko slammed into the wall of the pack house, using it to stop his momentum. He bent over, hands on his legs, panting from the effort and his frustration. His cock was just as hard as a few minutes ago and no amount of physical exertion was going to get rid of it.

Niko slipped quietly inside even though it was unlikely anyone was here this late. Another thing he'd have to adjust to if he was going to live his life as a human. Christ, he hadn't needed to keep daylight hours since graduating from high school. Even then he'd been a night owl and missed morning classes more often than not. Wolves were nocturnal, but he wasn't a wolf anymore, so he'd better get used to getting up at dawn and sleeping at night.

He headed for the shower already stroking his hard-on. He'd have to settle for living out his fantasies of dominating Zara, making her come and come and come, with his own hand around his cock. Getting those ideas out of his system before he went to see her at the hospital was imperative, and impossible.

The Zara he'd left eight years ago to do his duty to his family and all wolfkind, was a soft and naïve teenager who'd given him her virginity. Hell, he'd been just as young and inexperienced back then. A couple of years with the Volkovs had changed all that.

She would always be his shining angel of innocence. He could imagine the slap across the face she'd give him for even suggesting she let him tie her up, spank her curvy ass, pull her hair, all while making her pussy sing with want and need.

No. His Zara might get as dirty as allowing him to go

down on her, but she was a missionary style partner. Thus, Niko would be, too. A vanilla human life was what would help him to start over.

He'd keep both of them safe and protected in the staid existence of non-supernatural everyday living. No more wolves for her, no more wolf for him.

That's what he wanted. It's what he needed.

Somehow, he'd convince himself of that because, as far as he could tell, being a boring, middle-class, average citizen was his only choice to stay sane and alive. Plus, Zara had been through more than enough excitement for most humans' entire lives. This would be what was best for her, too.

For her, he could do it. He could be ordinary.

CRAZY

These days there wasn't much Zara was sure of, but she did know one thing. Mental hospitals were the worst. The place she was in now was so uninspiring that she couldn't even make a joke about how it sucked, and not in the good way. Pale blue walls, feelings groups, and paint your trauma, certainly weren't helping her get better.

She probably should have checked herself into a place like this a long time ago. No. That wasn't true. She'd done a perfectly fine job holding her hallucinations at bay for years. Stress triggered her episodes, and she'd learned the art of self-medicating through cupcakes and movie binges real fast. Meditation helped too, but not as well as chocolate ganache frosting on a batch of Heli's homemade cake balls.

There was one other thing that treated her self-diagnosed schizophrenia, keeping the crazy from controlling her life. She'd sooner admit she occasionally had conversations with imaginary rainbow dragons than let anyone know that she fantasized about her ex-boyfriend doing dirty, naughty things to her. Her high school sweetheart no less.

Kinky fantasies where he tied her up and bit her and sent her screaming into subspace had gotten her through more than a few stressful times. She got squirmy even thinking about it.

But now that Niko was back in town, she had to keep a tight lid on those kinds of thoughts. They were completely inappropriate. Especially for a woman like her, who'd been trafficked by some very bad people.

Her captors hadn't sexually assaulted her, unless her craze-ball hallucinations had also blocked a trauma like that from her consciousness. But the doctors didn't find any signs of abuse to her body after the rescue. Which was why she was in a mental hospital and not a regular one.

She had a few bumps and bruises that weren't going to heal overnight, but it was the world of make-believe she'd invented to block out the real memories of what happened that would keep her here.

Seriously? Werewolves?

That's what her mind had come up with to explain the bad things that were happening to her and around her... Freaking werewolves. She'd read one too many paranormal romance novels for her brain to have conjured up that baloney. At least it hadn't been vampires.

The only reason they didn't have her in a padded room drooling from a whole host of drugs was because she was calm, cool, and collected. She'd dealt with her strange fugue-state-like hallucinations for eight years and no one had ever been the wiser. None of her mental breakdowns had ever been quite as elaborate as this time. But she'd also never been kidnapped before either.

She discussed a course of treatment with the doctors that

included planned outpatient services as soon as she felt ready. She knew her rights and was good at advocating for them. No one would scare her into admitting herself into any long-term psychiatric care without demonstrating that she was a danger to herself or others.

Two or three days in the hospital was her limit. She was going home. Maybe today, maybe not. But by tomorrow definitely. While she was fully aware she needed to take care of her mental health, she had bigger fish to fry. Namely that evil bastard Ramsey Crescent.

Oh yeah, he was going to fry.

In the electric chair.

Not only had he kidnapped Zara and dragged her across state lines, he had a whole mess of other women held prisoner in his fancy-pants mansion in Cape Cod. Women who were slated to be mated to Crescent pack wolves.

Wait... No. That was part of the story her mind had made up. Zara clenched her fists and dug her nails into her hands trying to see past the blurred psychotic memories of witches and wolves and war.

"Zara, sweetie? Are you okay?" Heli's voice filtered in and broke through the dark clouds of memory. A soft hand touched her tight fist and helped bring her back to reality.

Zara opened her eyes and smiled at her younger sister. "I'm fine. Just concentrating on getting better as fast as possible."

"That's strange, because you looked as if you were about to throw up." Their friend and roommate, Galyna, stood a smidge behind Heli with a frown on her face. "I should warn you, I can scent emotions, and you smell like a little white lie."

What a funny thing to say. Especially since Gal was the

one who smelled... different. Zara pulled the thin blanket up and tucked it in around her, so they didn't see her free-boobing it in this flimsy hospital gown. "I think you're smelling your upper lip. I'm as fresh as a daisy."

She'd showered and everything this morning. A long, long, achingly hot shower. The sort that turned her skin red, but didn't wash away the real filth. The filth that was on the inside needed a different kind of cleansing, from the soul out. Not something she was going to get at this hospital.

The longer she was here, the worse that feeling would be for all those other women still in captivity. Yeah. She was getting out today. "I'm all ready to go home. You two didn't leave the house too much of a pigsty, did you?"

Heli and Gal exchanged worried looks. "You're coming home already? Is that what the doctors said? Shouldn't you give yourself some time?"

"I can rest at home just as well as here." Not that she was going to sit back and binge Netflix and eat gallons of ice cream or something. No, she had a lot of research to do on how to get away with murder. "I have no doubt you two will make sure I take it easy."

Criminal law wasn't her forte. She'd spent her time at the attorneys' offices of Gardner, Gilmartin, and Ginsburg working on civil rights, not defending bad guys. She'd gotten into law to help the underserved, underprivileged, and underappreciated. She knew everything there was to know about mergers and acquisitions, some really boring crap about employment rules, and a smidge about commercial leases, but not much about justifiable homicide. That was outside of her schooling.

Gal faked a smile. Why would she do that? Nerves. "Uh,

I'm happy to come over and hang out with you, but I moved in with Max a few weeks ago."

"Oh. That's great. I'm glad to see you guys hit it off." What Zara really wanted to say was something along the lines of - are you effing kidding me? The last thing she had seen of the two of them was some hot and heavy flirting. To have gone all love-at-first-sight was nuts.

Kind of like Zara. She wasn't one to chastise. She'd fallen for Niko the second she saw him jogging across the football field toward her. Silly teenage hormones. Galyna was a grown woman with a postgraduate degree. Maybe Heli could talk some sense into her.

Zara shrugged like it was no big deal one of her only friends was leaving her behind. "Aww, but you'll miss Heli's late-night quadruple chocolate chip cookies."

"Umm..." Heli shuffled her feet.

"Umm, what? Not you and Kosta. You swore that was just about the sex." Her sister was leaving her now too? Great... Fan-freaking-tastic... Fine. She didn't need anyone to take care of her. Never had.

Heli tried to reach for Zara's hand again, but would have had to dig deep into the blankets to get to her. "A lot has happened since then. Kosta and I are mated. I guess I thought you'd have seen that at the battle, but there was so much happening, maybe not."

The battle.

Her vision turned fuzzy around the edges, and her skin went clammy. She didn't want to talk about that now. In her mind, Kosta and Ramsey Crescent had shifted into were-wolves, along with a whole lot of other people, and fought almost to the death. The only person who'd been there that hadn't become a slathering beast was Niko.

Seeing him was as much of a shock as... well, the entire last month of her life. Niko had loved her and left her. That in and of itself was enough to send her into her first psychotic episode. Night after night she'd seen visions of him. Sometimes he was running through snowy woods dressed all in fur, other times he was in a dark club, drinking and dancing with women much more beautiful and sexual than she'd been at nineteen. She'd held it together then and had mostly been able to ignore the sights, sounds, and scents of her hallucinations.

She absolutely refused to have schizophrenia, paraphrenia, hyperphrenia, or any other -phrenia. If she did, she wasn't going to allow it to ruin her life. Zara defeated it back then, she could do it again.

The visions had been much too real to call them daydreams, or even nightmares. There were so many times she was sure she could reach out and touch him, feel him, be there with him. That was when she'd looked up schizophrenia and made the decision that there was no way she could tell anyone what was happening.

Not even her parents. They both worked so hard to do so much good in the world, that having to deal with the way her teenage brain had decided to cope with the breakup would have been a waste of their energy. She'd handled it on her own and learned to become a productive member of society all on her own. She made sure to do plenty of civil rights pro bono work to keep from allowing lawyering to suck her soul away.

She hadn't made it through an Ivy League university and law school all on her own. Her family was there every step of the way. It had taken a whole heck of a lot of meditation and yoga classes with her mom, long discussions about constitutional law with her dad as they walked through the Reserve, romance novels, and her sister's regular care-packages filled with cupcakes to beat back the stress she knew had to be causing her mind to show her things that weren't there. None of them had known how much they helped.

Which was more than she could ever say about Niko.

"Knock, knock." Speak of the handsome devil.

What the heck was he doing here? Not only had she thought he would be in the hospital himself, and for a good long time, but he wasn't supposed to be in her room. She'd never said he could visit her.

"Hey, Niko." Heli stepped in front of Niko and gave him a huge hug. "It's really great to see you out and about."

Galyna darted over to Zara's bed, whipped off the cute pink cardigan she was wearing and thrust it out at her, shaking it like it was an emergency that Zara put it on. It was better than the faded blue-ish, slightly see-through hospital gown. She supposed pulling the blanket up over her head and yelling at Niko to go away wouldn't show the doctors she was ready to be an outpatient.

Zara grabbed the sweater, shoved her arms into it, and buttoned it all the way up. She smoothed her hair and Galyna handed her a shiny lip gloss. Gal winked at her and moved a stray strand of hair, giving her locks a little fluff. "Sorry, I don't have any concealer or mascara. I'd say give your cheeks a pinch for some color, but they're already pink."

No, they were not. Okay, fine. They totally were. Zara didn't want to feel anything for the rat bastard who'd moved a billion miles away right after he'd asked her to marry him. If she had a ring to throw in his face, she would. Then she'd smother him with kisses... Then she'd slap him... Then dry hump his leg while shoving her tongue down his throat.

Gah. Maybe she did need to stay in the mental hospital.

Niko finally was able to side-step Heli, and he held out a small sprig of bamboo in a tiny vase filled with rocks and water. "I got you this. Thought you might want something living in a place like this."

Dammit. Why was he so thoughtful and astute? Probably a suggestion from his mother. She was a well-bred, classy lady. "Thanks. You didn't have to bring me anything."

"I've got an awful lot of making up to do with you. A little plant is the least I can do."

Zara swallowed and set the vase on the side table next to her medications. Her hands didn't even shake.

Niko glanced at Galyna and Heli and shoved his thumbs into his pockets. He looked like he was going to say something but didn't. An uncomfortable silence filled the room until Zara wanted to scream. She kept it in though. Instead, she cleared her throat.

Heli took the cue. "You seem to be all healed up from the battle. Kosta said your wolves could do that faster than in human form."

"Uh, yeah, They can... I didn't–"

Zara's heart rate shot up so high that if she was still hooked up to the monitors, they'd be sounding the alarm. "Wolves?"

Did they know? No, they couldn't. She hadn't even told the psychiatrist she'd hallucinated that her captors had been werewolves. Bile burned the back of Zara's throat. "Why would you have wolves, Niko? Did you bring them back from Russia? I think that's illegal."

His eyes went wide, and he took a step away. "No, I definitely didn't bring a wolf back with me."

He turned to Heli and Gal. "I... I thought..."

"So did we. I don't understand. Maybe I should get Doc."

"No... It's okay. I'm fine. No wolves." She shouldn't have said anything. Her hard work of pretending to be sane was slipping away and being replaced by the awful buzzing in her hears. "It's fine. Don't mind me."

"Zara?" Heli tipped her head to the side. "How much do you remember about the Crescent pack and your time there?"

Pack. Heli had just called the people living with Ramsey Crescent a pack. No, no, no, no. That couldn't be.

Oh, shitballs. She must be hallucinating. Again. Right now. That had to be why she couldn't breathe except in small gulps.

Zara glanced at Niko, and while he looked worried, his face was one-hundred percent human. But Heli's eyes were glowing purple, and Galyna was sprouting fur and a snout.

"Nothing. I don't remember anything." She didn't want to. "I swear."

Also... her pants were currently on fire.

FIFTY FIRST DATES

*W*ho better to turn to when life threw FUBAR situations his way, such as Zara not remembering wolfkind, than his mother? Not like he'd gotten a choice. Selena Troika watched Niko with the fierce eyes of the wolftress she was. When he'd come home from seeing his ex-girlfriend in the hospital, she'd attacked him with questions.

"Nikolai, something has happened, and if you try to keep it from me, you will be sorry, young man."

Up until now, his mother had given him a wide berth. She blamed herself for getting him involved in the revolution. He knew better. Even if Selena hadn't been a revolutionary, Niko was destined to change their world anyway. He'd known that since the first day he'd seen Zara and fallen for her on the spot.

His mother had always been on his side, more than anyone ever realized. She could be his ally again in his fight to win his true mate back. "I've been to see Zara at the hospital."

Selena grabbed his arm, worried. "Doc said she was recovering well just last night. Has something happened? Will she be okay?"

"I need your help, Mom. With Zara." That was easier to say out loud than expected. He'd never talked to anyone about his feelings for Zara.

Wolf law had been pounded into his head from an early age. He had to believe in and uphold the Volkovs' edicts to keep his pack and all wolf shifters around the world safe. That meant never letting humans know they existed. His parents, especially his father, had been opposed to him dating a human. His mother relented first and had let up on her persistent matchmaking.

Now he understood why.

She never intended him to be strategically mated to a wolftress from another pack. Selena Troika was a romantic and wanted better for her sons. She'd schemed most of their lives so they could find and fall in love with their true mates.

Fated mates wasn't just a fairy tale matriarchs told their young pups. The damn Volkovs had ruined it by declaring mating anyone but another wolf shifter illegal. With the death of the Black Prince, the last English ruler with werewolf blood, wolfkind was no longer protected and the church began to target supernatural beings in earnest. Werewolves had been hunted almost to extinction. By secluding the survivors into packs far from humans, forbidding any contact, they had preserved their race.

But that was more than seven hundred years ago. Progress back into society had been too slow. Christ, his grandfather's generation were the first to interact with humans at all. Even that had been a hard-fought battle. Worth it though.

"Just warning you, the answer is probably more orgasms." She raised her eyebrows in a sort of can-you-handle-this way.

Oh, God. "Mother."

"What?" She gave him a gallic shrug. "I'm not wrong."

No, she wasn't. But... eww. He didn't want sex advice. "This problem might need more than, uh, that."

She nodded sagely. "Great sex."

Why, oh why, did his mom have sex on the brain? This was serious. "Zara doesn't even want me anywhere near her. How am I going to win her back when–"

Selena clapped her hands. "Finally, you've decided to come back to the land of the living. If you're in, I can work with just about anything. We need a plan. How about–"

Niko had no doubt his mother had plans on top of plans wrapped around plans. She didn't have all the details though, and he probably should have led with the most important information. He couldn't even believe it himself. "She doesn't remember. Anything"

Not much made Selena Troika go silent. This news did. She opened her mouth to say something and then closed it. She raised one finger as if to ask a clarifying question and then huffed. "Nothing? Like *Fifty First Dates?*"

"Not exactly. She doesn't have any memories of being kidnapped or anything that happened pretty much all of the last month. She didn't even know I was back, and she has no idea about wolfkind."

"Well, shit." She plopped onto the couch across from him and frowned for a good long time. "Neither Gal nor Heli knew about our true natures before they got with your brothers, so that part I can work with. I'm more concerned that she's blocked out the entire trauma. I'd like to talk to Doc about that."

"Yeah. Me, too. But I don't want to ever lie to her again." Leaving Zara was the second worst night of his life. His father convinced him that breaking up with her was for the best. He'd be serving the Wolf Tzar in Russia for several long years, and it wasn't fair to ask her to wait for him. He wasn't allowed to take her as a mate anyway. Or so he'd thought.

He wouldn't think about that now.

"Listen, *sinochek*. I'll work on what to do about Zara's missing memories, but you've got to get on that girl's radar outside of the hospital. Take her out, wine and dine her. Help her remember what's important."

"What is important?" He used to know, but his own judgement wasn't to be trusted.

His mother touched his cheek. "Why she loved you in the first place."

Shit. That wasn't going to work. He wasn't the same man he was before. No, if he was going to get Zara to fall for him again, it had to be a different Niko.

Not new and improved, because he certainly wasn't better than before. The only thing left from the alpha he used to be was his determination to make her fall for him. That made his mom's advice moot.

Except maybe the sex part. Not that he'd be talking to his mother about that again... Ew... Just ew.

Niko pulled her hand from his face and gave it a pat. "Thanks for the advice, Mom."

"Oh, no." She shook her head. "You're going to go ask your brothers for manly advice now, aren't you?"

Now that was a good idea. "I think I'll head over to the Sleepy Folk and see what Max is doing."

Selena rolled her eyes at him, but she was hiding a smile too. Niko kissed her on the head and realized that was the first time he'd shown anyone any affection since he'd gotten back. This was also the longest conversation he'd had in months.

The darkness in his soul pushed back against this new forward movement he'd made. His vision blurred and his heart pounded against his chest, trying to break free of the pain inside.

What he needed was a drink.

Max was behind the bar when Niko snuck in through the back door, and he definitely looked surprised as shit to see him. Fair enough. This was the first time he'd been to the Sleepy Folk during open hours. Certainly not when there were lots of people around. They would want to talk to him, ask him how he was.

His vision tunneled around the edges, and he consciously beat it back until he could see normally again. He could do this. He could do this. He could be a normal person.

Niko sauntered across the room and waved at his brother, like this was any other average day, and headed toward the bar. "Hey. I thought I might help out behind the scenes, you know restocking and stuff, tonight. I haven't really done much since I got back, and I'd like to fix that."

"Huh. Okay. Cool." Max slapped him on the shoulder, but a flash of worry went through his eyes too. "Happy to have you here. You should know, Gal is upstairs at the pie shop with Zara. I'm pretty sure they'll head down here next. Sort of Zara's reintroduction into real life."

Max glanced over Niko's shoulder toward the stairs that led down into the speakeasy with all the love in the world written across his face. That look was reserved for his mate and tugged at the darkness in Niko. He would never begrudge his brother the joy Gal brought to him. Hell, he'd sacrificed his life so that Max could mate whoever he wanted.

Niko ignored the black mark on his soul for hating his brother's happiness and turned to see the ladies coming down to the bar, even though he wasn't ready. His gut clenched, and he was this damn close to hurling.

Yeah, that was a great way to make a good impression on Zara. Fuck. Just watching her descend the stairs had his brain and his body at war with each other.

His cock wanted him to walk over there and sweep her off her feet. Literally. He'd throw her over his shoulder caveman style, drag her to the back room, tie her down so she was on her knees for him, and make her cry out his name in pleasure as he did all the dirty and delicious things he was dying to do.

Niko wasn't a wolf. He was a pig.

He'd better serve the people around him as bacon than an alpha. Hold up… Where had that idea come from? He wasn't an alpha. Not anymore. Niko had resigned himself to that. He was lucky to be alive, and shouldn't be even thinking he could lead his own pack. A broken piece of shit like him wasn't fit to lead a granny across the street, much less his fellow wolf shifters.

Still, the thought that he was supposed to be an alpha had popped into his head. Almost like someone had placed it there, waiting for him to let it jump into the front of his mind.

Nope. No good could come from going down that road. Maybe someday, when he'd figured out how to get his wolf back, he'd consider joining the Troika Pack's Enforcers again. He couldn't count on ever being able to shift gain, and now that Zara didn't remember anything about the wolves who'd taken her, it was best that he couldn't.

Yeah. Taking care of her was a better goal than worrying about being a fucking alpha. The Troikas had their leader. Max led the wolves in Rogue well. He was strong, he was smart, and he cared. Plus, he had his eyes firmly facing the future.

That's all Niko had ever wanted. To see the Troikas leave the antiquated ways of the past behind so their wolves could choose their own paths to happiness.

That was enough.

Almost.

Another thought rose up unbidden, as if whispered into his subconscious. There was one more thing he'd always wanted and had denied himself.

The light scent of her skin, perfumed with the sweetest of brown sugar, cinnamon, and apples, with her own touch of something soft and clean, like a fluffy cloud drifted over his senses. This afternoon, for the first time since he'd gone on the run into the cold Russian night, Niko had experienced an emotion other than regret, disdain, and hatred.

Just being in the same room as Zara for all of a minute and forty-seven seconds had done that. He'd denied the reaction when he'd gone to the hospital. He was too wound up about seeing her for the first time, he wasn't sure what he'd been feeling. He'd made a stupid excuse to get the hell out of there before they even got to talk.

This time he wasn't going anywhere. He wanted Zara. He wanted more. So much more.

His mind raced round and round between hoping that being near her would be good for him, and knowing his own darkness could bring her down into his murky self-hatred. He would not do that to her. Not even to save himself.

Maybe the tiniest of interactions would be enough to sustain him for a little while. He could just say hello, bring her a tasty beverage. He was part owner of the bar after all.

He didn't even know what Zara liked to drink. Was she a martini girl? Shots didn't seem her style. Beer? Was he completely overthinking this? Yes... Yes, he was. He'd make her an old fashioned. There was something stylish and sophisticated about it and the sweet almond flavor of smooth whiskey reminded him of her kisses.

Goddess, her kisses. His mouth watered, and he saw stars for a second just thinking about touching his lips to hers, tangling their tongues, and hearing her soft little moans when he teased her in all the ways she loved.

He really needed to get his mind out of the gutter, or he was going to have to hide behind the bar for the entire night to keep the fucking tent in his pants from scaring away the rest of the patrons. His scowl would do the trick anyway. He took a couple of deep breaths and concentrated on creating the perfect drink.

He selected just the right glasses, splashed his dash of bitters over the sugar cubes, found perfectly square blocks of ice, poured an eye-measured amount of whiskey over each, and dropped in the curls of orange zest. It took most of his concentration. Through every single step he kept Zara in the corner of his eye.

She sat at a table with Galyna, and while her friend was clearly elated to see her, Zara kept her arms folded around herself and her eyes flitted about as if looking for something or someone.

That churning in his gut returned. Was she here for a date?

Niko may not have his wolf, but he'd still rip the throat out of any man who touched her. He didn't even like his own brothers smiling at her. One more way he was clearly a pig. He couldn't have Zara, but he sure as shit didn't want anyone else to.

P.

I.

G.

She wasn't a possession.

She wasn't his.

Even though every cell in his body screamed *mine.*

Niko picked up the two drinks he'd made and swallowed each in a gulp. It would take a hell of a lot more than a couple of shots of whiskey to get him drunk. A couple of bottles might do it.

He'd been on that route. Drinking his way into oblivion was difficult for a shifter. Damn metabolisms were too fast. The little bit of numbness from drinking a shit-ton of hard alcohol was nothing compared to a single night spent fantasizing about Zara. Both were torture, one sweet and one bitter.

Okay. Fine. He was going to talk to her. Not about anything specific. He'd just say hi. He knew better than to ask how she was. He hated it when people asked how he was doing. She'd been through her own battles. If she was lucky, she'd come through it all without the scars he had.

If he was really lucky, he could help her get through it. They'd fight their demons together.

Niko made the old fashions again and walked toward the table where she and Gal sat. He could do this and not make a complete ass of himself. Probably.

"Hey. Thought you two looked thirsty." Suave, he was not. But he hadn't sounded like a total douchepotato. He set the drinks down, one in front of each of the ladies.

Zara's eyes went wide and she grabbed the cocktail in front of Galyna. She stared at it for a second like it was a ticking time bomb and then downed the whole thing in two hard gulps.

"Okay," Gal said warily. "I guess this one is mine."

"No," Zara practically shouted and snatched up the second glass, downing it a little too fast so that dribbles of the drink ran down the sides of her mouth. She grimaced and then burped. 'Sorry. I was thirsty."

Or an alcoholic. Geez. "Uh. I can make you another one, Gal."

Zara stood up, grabbed wrist and said, "I'll help."

Her touch sent surges of heat through every inch of his skin. He bit the inside of his cheek to keep from wrapping his arms around her just to feel her warmth on his cold, damned soul. Instead, he let her lead him across the place and back to the hallway toward the supply room. Whoa. Where was she taking him and why?

She dragged him straight into the place where he'd imagined having her on her knees for him only a few moments before, and his cock came springing to life.

He hadn't gotten hard like this without a lot of spit and stroking in a long time, before tonight. Now he was on hard-on number two within the span of five minutes. At least he knew the fucking thing still had some life in it. "Zara, where are we going?"

"To get some bottles of water. You can't let Galyna drink any alcohol."

"Sweetheart, we have water behind the bar." The second he called her that, he knew it was a mistake.

She dropped his arm and shook her hand. "Why is your skin so hot? And don't call me that. I haven't been your sweetheart for a long time."

She would always be his sweetheart. Niko mentally gagged at his own syrupy thoughts. Zara wasn't his at all. No matter how much he thought she should be. Wait... That didn't come out how he meant it to. No matter how much he wanted her to be.

Shit. Snort snort, fucking pig.

Add that to the list of his flaws because he did believe that she was his, all the way to his core.

Because if she let him back into her life, he would treasure her, pleasure her, and make sure she knew she was cherished. Not like he'd done a good job of that last time.

He needed to walk away right now. Screw the remnants of feelings he had for Zara, fuck the desire to take her and shove her up against the wall and scrape his teeth across her throat while he pinned her hands over her head.

He was so fucked.

FLIRTING AND OTHER DANGEROUS GAMES

"*N*iko?" His eyes had gone all dark and then he'd gotten this blank sort of absent look of shock on his face. She could totally relate. Whatever was wrong worried her. Schizophrenia wasn't contagious, so it had to be something else distracting him.

He blinked and swallowed. "Huh?"

"Bottled water? For Galyna."

"Right." Niko led her back toward the bar, but paused at the end of the hallway. He quirked his head to the side like a puppy, wondering what she was thinking. "Why can't she have a drink?"

Crapballs. He wasn't supposed to ask questions. Zara needed to be more careful about how and who she interacted with. Her brain played too many tricks on her to keep things straight.

"I can't tell you." Because Niko did not need to see how batshit crazy she was. She couldn't exactly say she'd had a vision of Gal pregnant. With twins. The whole idea was incredibly dumb. Believing it was true was extra stupid. Making a fuss and dragging Niko into it was beyond foolish.

If she was going to convince everyone that she was safe enough not be in the hospital and make sure they weren't keeping tabs on her all the time, she'd have to be better at hiding her reactions to what her mind told her was real. Gal was not pregnant with twins. Standing here in a hallway with a sexy man was.

Niko stepped into her space and stared down into her eyes. "You can tell me anything. If you can't talk to me, who can you?"

His muscles bunched in his arms as if he was about to wrap her up in them. He clenched his hands into fists and shoved them into his pockets.

What would it be like to be snuggled up in his warm embrace again? To confide in the one man she used to share all her hopes and dreams with? For just a minute she'd love to unburden herself and let him take care of her.

She could never do that.

"I don't think so. Just because we dated in high school doesn't mean anything." Whoa. Was that really how she felt? He wasn't some ex-boyfriend from high school. They'd been engaged. For like twenty minutes. Then they'd gone and told his parents and within the hour, they were no longer allowed to even see each other.

A week later he'd left for to Russia. Rush-uhh, for goodness sake. Zara had never thought she'd see him again. The way his dad made it sound, he was basically emigrating. Maybe that had simply been a ploy to make her let go of him up easier.

She had given him up. It hadn't been easy. She didn't want

to go through all of that heart pain more than once. Not with him, not with any man. Besides, she had other things to take care of in which she wasn't going to involve him or anyone else she loved.

Shoot. She hadn't meant that. She didn't love Niko.

Very much.

Until she found a way to mete out justice on Ramsey Crescent, she couldn't afford to have feelings. Maybe once she'd killed him, put a final stop to his human trafficking schemes, and rescued the rest of the women he'd taken, then she could think about moving on with her own life.

"Zara. I can't change what happened. I wish I could go back and do a lot of things very differently. I am so damn sorry for hurting you." There was the tiniest tremble in his voice that tugged at her heart strings, playing a tune she didn't want to hear right now.

She only had so much emotional bandwidth and taking down Ramsey Crescent had to take all of her focus. "Coming here tonight was a mistake. I can't do this."

The back door to the bar called to her from the end of the hallway they stood in and it made a convenient escape. She could easily walk home. The little house she used to share with Heli and Gal was only a short distance from Rogue's historic old town district. She'd be fine on her own. "I gotta go."

She darted down the hall, pushed out the back door, and stepped into the cool night air. The door shut behind her with a click, and she closed her eyes, taking in a long, slow breath. One more minute in close quarters with Niko, and she was either going to slap him for no good reason or kiss him for a million bad ones.

It would be best if she didn't see him again. Like ever. An uncomfortable hollow opened up around her heart. Fine. That was better than the fear of him seeing her mental instability or exposing him to the dangers of her plan to take down Ramsey Crescent.

No, it was best to tackle both of those things alone. Starting right now.

Zara took one step into the dark alley and then heard the door open behind her.

"Don't move a muscle, *solnyshka*. You aren't walking home alone. I'll go with you and keep you safe."

Sigh... She'd be mad if that protectiveness and possessiveness wasn't incredibly sexy. She was a strong, independent woman for goodness sake. She didn't need a big bad man to keep her safe.

Except, she really liked knowing he was there with her. Eye roll to herself. "What took you so long?"

He chuckled softly under his breath and stepped up beside her. "Sorry. I went to tell Gal not to worry because I was taking you home."

"She gave you a high five for that, huh?" Zara didn't need psychotic visions or even psychic ones to have a clear picture of that happening.

The twinkle in his eye, the one that made her legs go wobbly, told her everything she needed to know. He gave her nose a little boop. "Maybe."

The teenage part of her said to swat his hand away. The weary grown-up said it was cute, and she should take all the affection she could get before she went and screwed up the rest of her life. Because there would be no nose boops in jail...

or hell. Whichever was the consequence for killing a very bad man. "Why is everyone conspiring against me?"

She loved that Gal was happy for her and Niko to get back together, which might be partially a product of Gal dating Niko's younger brother. Her friend probably privy to more of what had been happening in Niko's world than she was. Fine. That didn't bother her. Much.

What she didn't want was for everyone to worry about her. That meant they would be watching her, and she needed to do a better job of making them think everything was back to normal.

Niko slid his hand into hers and gave it a squeeze. "Maybe we're conspiring for you."

The hollow in her chest from a few minutes before filled in with a warmth she remembered from a long time ago, in a galaxy far, far away. He didn't need to know that she secretly craved his touch and wanted him to put his hands all over her. Nope... Definitely not. "I'm not dignifying that with a response."

"Come on, let's get you home and tucked into bed." He slipped a strand of hair behind her ear, and his eyes flashed to her lips and then up to her eyes.

Was that... no. Even if it was an offer to take her to bed, she wasn't letting him into the house, much less into her pants or her heart. She pretended not to notice the innuendo in his sentence and stared straight ahead, at his wide chest and big ole muscles. Eep. Maybe that wasn't the right place to focus her attention. Too tempting.

As much as she still felt the old hurts and had some unresolved anger at him for leaving, it would be so easy to fall into

Niko's arms and let him take care of her, take care of everything. Now that he was back, the whole town probably expected them to pick up where they left off. Obviously, her friends did.

She doubted his parents wanted that. Well, she'd save them the worry. She'd already committed herself to a different path that only included helping those who couldn't help themselves. Starting with the women in the Crescent stronghold. The sooner she found Ramsey Crescent and his weaknesses, the better.

They walked toward the Reserve in silence. This time it wasn't awkward, but an underlying tension zinged between the two of them, a lot like before a first kiss. That wasn't something she'd experienced in far too long. Zara absorbed every little bit of joy she could get out of the moment. She would be denying herself any more than that, starting as soon as possible, so this had to sustain her for a good while.

She would dig into those plans tomorrow. There were a few things to research and some paperwork to do to make sure no one else in her family could be held liable for her actions or lose anything if she were to get caught. The law would not look kindly on her taking justice into her own hands, but that couldn't be helped.

Just in case she did get away with it, she needed to set up some kind of foundation, a 501(c)3 non-profit to help not only the women Crescent had trafficked, but others like them. Zara wasn't going to stand for anyone treating women with such blatant hatred and disregard. She'd become an angel of death if necessary.

"I'd love to know what's got your big ole brain whirling right now." Niko stopped them on the sidewalk where the path split. One way led to the walking trails that crisscrossed the Reserve and the other skirted the outside of the park. The open space closed at dusk and most people followed that rule. There were long held rumors of wolves running around in the forest, even though local law enforcement denied it.

Wolves. Goosebumps rose up all across her skin and she shivered. Why did it have to be wolves? "Nothing important, just thinking about all the things I need to do tomorrow."

Niko led her toward the path that went straight into the dark forest like they were on a light and breezy summer walk. "Want help?"

"No." The cracking of a twig sounded from somewhere behind them. Big dangerous predators or her imagination? "What was that?"

Niko glanced in the direction of the sound and smiled softly, pulling her along the dirt trail, not giving any danger a thought. "Nothing to be nervous about. I got you. You're safe with me."

Her eyes darted everywhere waiting for the visions to flitter in. This was exactly the kind of situation that would spike her stress levels. She'd start seeing monsters any second now. She hated that her knees and voice were both trembling. "You're not worried about the wild animals that live here and hunt in the dark?"

"Not even a little." Niko pulled her into his side, wrapping one arm around her shoulders protectively.

God, to have his complete confidence. Especially in the face of evil, dark forests filled with creepy beasts who wanted to eat their faces. The only reason she wasn't a slathering mess of nerves curled into a little ball was his total lack of fear. She drew on it and shivered a bit less inside. "Why not?"

He winked at her. "I can't tell you."

Oh, come on. Maybe she let the very edges of her mouth turn up in a grin. "You said we could tell each other anything."

"No." He poked her in the shoulder. "I said you could tell me anything. You didn't."

"You're infuriating." She was not going to giggle and flirt with her ex-boyfriend. Not even a little bit. Instead, she scowled at him. Hard. "I don't remember you being such a smartass, smartass."

He scowled back, and it was so fake, she almost laughed out loud. He must have noticed because he narrowed his eyes even more. "Oh. I always was. I just tempered it for you."

Yeah right. He was yanking her chain. "I don't believe that for a second."

"You don't? Well, fuck. I guess I gotta up my game for you,"

That actually made her laugh for real this time. He was being adorably cute and yet totally sexy at the same time. "You're a schmoe."

He stopped and brushed his lips across her forehead. "You're home."

Wait... What? Sure enough, they were standing on the sidewalk in front of her house. He'd distracted her with his horrible flirting for the entire walk through the deep dark forest with all the mean beasties. "Oh. Umm. Thanks."

She shuffled her feet. Niko was actually a good guy who smelled so scrummy, and she longed to invite him in. She couldn't though. Because she'd jump his bones.

That was not part of the plan. Niko was throwing a serious wrench in said plan. Just being around him was making her think about a different life. She wanted to pretend all of their past history was just that... history. They could wrap themselves up in each other and be perfectly happy reigniting the flame that was only banked inside of her.

But then there were those women that needed her help. So, no. She wasn't going to ask him to come in. Not into her house, not into her life. No matter how much her soul begged her too.

"Thanks for walking me home." Zara glanced up at Niko, kind of expecting him to be surprised at the rebuff since they'd been having fun a moment before. He wasn't even looking at her. Something else had caught his attention and whatever it was, wasn't good.

"Don't move, *solnyshka*. Don't look in the house. Just pretend we're flirting and having a good old time. Laugh at what I'm saying and touch my arm."

Oh shit... Oh shitty shit. Not only was Niko freaking her the hell out, his eyes were glowing with an amber light from within. She gulped and did what he'd said. Zara grabbed his arm, right at the bicep and gave it a squeeze. "Ha ha ha. You're so funny."

"Good girl. I'm going to kiss you and then we're walking away all hurried like we can't wait to get in each other's pants. We'll go toward the Troika house. Okay? Ready?"

Kiss? At a time like this? She didn't even understand what was wrong. "No."

"Too bad, I'm coming in. At least pretend to enjoy it." If his tone wasn't so serious this would almost be funny.

Zara's teeth were suddenly incredibly dry, and she couldn't seem to swallow. She darted her tongue out to lick her lips like a weird fish-mouth kisser. That's exactly when Niko's mouth touched hers. Her tongue was already doing its own thing, without her permission and licked along the seam of his lips.

Niko groaned so low, it was almost a growl, and opened for her, teasing her tongue with his. He shoved his hands into her hair and clenched the strands so tight it pulled at her scalp. The sensation sent her whole body tingling. He broke the kiss way before she was ready.

Really loudly, he said, "Come on, babe. My car is just around the corner. The back seat is calling our names."

He made the play-along face and stretched one eyebrow toward her house. Oh. Ohhh. "Ooh, yes... I love me some back seat loving. Let's go... I can't wait."

Whoever Niko was trying to lay a false track for wasn't going to buy any of that. She sounded like a bad robot in a D-grade horror movie. Bugger. They were so getting murdered.

Probably by werewolves if her luck held out.

LET'S MAKE A DEAL

*F*ucking hell.

Zara didn't remember anything about being kidnapped or her time in captivity and now her worst night-mare was standing five feet in front of them. Thinking about kissing her again wasn't helping. But good Goddess, what a kiss. The way she'd tasted him almost made his head explode... and he didn't mean the one above his shoulders.

Now was not the fucking time. He planned on a hell of a lot more kissing, and hopefully more, later. As soon as he got them far, far away from the asshole stalking her. What the fuck was Ramsey Crescent doing in her house and how had the Troika enforcers not taken him down for being in their territory in the first place?

He and Zara were getting out of here right now. When had her to safety, maybe tucked away in the pack house with his mother and a half-dozen wolftress enforcers as guards, he was coming back here... and what? It wasn't like he could fight Crescent. His human form was as weak as, well, a human. All

Crescent would have to do was shift one claw and take a swipe at him.

That little fact had been proven at the battle for Kosta's new pack. Niko would have gladly sacrificed his life to help his brother. He hadn't had anything to live for back then. Seeing Zara that night changed everything.

"Let's hurry." He tugged at Zara's arm, but made a major miscalculation. By doing so, he turned her so she got a direct view of her house. No time to stop. Hopefully her acting skills would improve in the next five seconds, and she could pretend she hadn't seen anything.

"Tell me I didn't just see the Incredible Hulk standing in my living room." She looked away a little too quickly and gasped.

Shit. Nope. She glanced over at him wide-eyed and then back at the big window at the front of the house. No way she'd missed green glowing eyes on the man in her living room. Zara tried to cover her surprise, but there was no mistake. She recognized Crescent. Seeing him must be bringing on bad memories.

Regardless, he wasn't going to let that beast anywhere near Zara. He broke into a run, being careful to keep pace she could match. "Do you know who that is?"

She shook her head. "No, should I?"

Niko's sense of smell wasn't what it was before he'd lost his wolf and he couldn't tell if she was lying or not. That was a new irritating discovery. He'd always been able to rely on scent to warn him of all kinds of emotions, which was especially handy when it came to the women in his life. One more thing to add to his checklist of how to be a normal human.

Even without scenting her fear, he could tell her adrenaline was spiking by the way the pulse point at her throat was beating so hard he could see it. Her breathing had ratcheted up, and her eyes had dilated. She was in fight, flight, or freeze response mode. Luckily, his flight response worked just fine.

Niko glanced over his shoulder to make sure Crescent wasn't in pursuit and begged the Goddess that some enforcers were nearby. Should they duck back into the Reserve? He knew its trees and bushes, rocks and streams like his own skin. He'd spent the first eighteen years of his life running free through the forest almost every night.

They could hide, but they wouldn't stay hidden long from a wolf like Crescent. He wasn't the alpha of the Crescent Bay pack just because of his name. He was a skilled hunter.

The Troika pack house was pretty close, especially if they cut through the Reserve. Hopefully, one of the Enforcer patrols would scent an intruder chasing them and come to the rescue. They were going to have to risk it.

"Hello, my naughty seer." The creeptastic voice of their enemy laid claimed to Zara's attention.

While Niko was being a dumbass and guarding their six, Ramsey Crescent had gotten the drop on them and popped out from behind a parked car on the street. No wolf worth his weight would have missed the scent of another shifter so close. He was going to have to put on one hell of a show to make sure the bastard didn't clue into his disability. The second this alpha discovered Niko couldn't shift, he'd take them both out.

"Get away from me, you disrespectful toad." Zara held out her hand like she could mow him down with the force of her mind, Luke Skywalker style.

Christ, she was gorgeous, on fire and valiant, like she was

going to protect him. She crushed his hand so tight in hers, he'd lose circulation in his fingers soon, and that made her all the more courageous because she was afraid and still wasn't backing down.

Niko squeezed her hand, so she knew he wasn't going anywhere. "Step off, Crescent. You don't belong here."

"Ah, the prodigal son, back from the dead... Again. I had hoped my enforcers would have wounded you gravely enough that your family would be grieving your death for real this time. You're a cockroach. One that I intend to–"

"Shut up, fucktard." Zara took a step toward Crescent.

That took the asshole by surprise. "Look at the mouth on you. If I'd known you were nasty like that I might have–"

"I said, shut up." Zara jerked like she was going to strike the guy.

As much as Niko would love to see his woman take this egotistical Cheeto down a few pegs, she didn't understand what he really was and how great of danger they were in. He pulled her behind him and stepped in front of her, even though he guessed that would piss her off. "You heard the lady. I'd suggest you do as you're told."

"Protect her all you want, but I will get her back," he snapped. His patience was wearing thin and that meant Niko and Zara didn't have much more time until Crescent's real attack would land.

Time to bluff. Niko lowered his head and glared at the other alpha. In a very deliberate and low voice he challenged. "You'll never touch her again."

His con paid off. Crescent paused before speaking. But he had something up his sleeve. Niko just didn't know what it was yet. Shit, he wished some Troika enforcers would get their asses over here.

Crescent paced one way and then another, taking his time responding. "Would you like to guarantee that, boy?"

Crescent was around the same age as Niko's father would have been, but Niko had learned not to let age intimidate him. "Good try, old man. You even think about Zara again and my pack will destroy you. We don't need any deal from you."

"I doubt that very much. Your pack is in complete disarray. It was child's play to walk right into your territory and into her house. Not an alpha or Enforcer in sight. You were so preoccupied with getting in her pants that you didn't even notice you were surrounded." Crescent pointed at Niko with one claw extended. Then he flicked his wrist and two of his wolves prowled up out of the shadows, another two came up the street from the direction of Zara's house, and still two more from behind parked cars.

Niko expected Zara to cry out or yell at the wolves or something. She didn't even flinch. It was like they were invisible to her. Perhaps because all of her focus was on Ramsey Crescent. He couldn't blame her for that.

He wished he couldn't see those wolves ready to attack either. If they survived this encounter, he was going to have a lot of explaining to do to her. He'd wanted to tell Zara about wolfkind since they were teenagers. Guess this was his big chance. "You're assuming my enforcers aren't here watching us right now. All they need is the signal from me and they'll destroy you."

"Will they? But not you? What do you have to say about that, seer?" Crescent addressed his last question to Zara.

That was the second instance of him calling her that. Why? What did he think Zara saw?

For the first time since Crescent and his wolves had shown up, Zara paled and lost some of her bravado. She opened her mouth, but no words came out. Only the tiniest of whimpers. The seer thing had gotten to her. Strange.

"I think your girlfriend is broken, Troika, or she's hiding her abilities from you. Either way, she has reason to be scared. This time I won't be so kind. Maybe she already knows that." Crescent smiled and tipped his head to the side, studying Zara and her reactions.

Niko shoved her fully behind him pinning her between his back and the nearest car. She wouldn't be able to see any more of this dickhead's manipulations. "Don't think for a second I will let you take her, Crescent."

He'd come up with some way to keep her safe. Please, Goddess. There had to be something he could do besides bluff. That could only last so long. Niko glanced down at the car windows hoping against hope he could punch through the glass on the door. Then what? Shove her inside to be trapped?

But... holy shit. The old-school pin locks weren't depressed. There they sat upright like little tin soldiers. Niko inched closer to the door's handle and grabbed Zara's hand, slipping her fingers under the metal. Her quiet intake of breath signaled that she understood his plan.

Niko simply had to keep Crescent busy enough that he wouldn't notice Zara pull that handle. Then they could both jump inside and lock the doors.

"I'll make you a deal, Troika." The alpha in Ramsey Crescent was coming out to play now.

Perfect. Keep talking, asshole. Whatever his reason for

being here was about to be revealed. If Niko was very, very lucky he could use Crescent's so-called deal to get Zara as far away as possible and to safety. "Oh, really? Do tell."

"You're outnumbered and out maneuvered, but I'm a fair alpha. I'll give you what you want," Crescent stared Niko right in the eye, then his gaze flashed to Zara and back again. "If you give me what I need."

Not a chance in heaven or hell. It was time for him to get Zara out of here. They'd have maybe a two second head start if they ran. More if he could shove her in this car and run over the bastard. This was one case where Niko didn't need his wolf. He'd learned how to hotwire a car from his human friends in high school. Thank the Goddess for his misspent youth. "What exactly is that?"

"I'm tired of this war and seeing our people divided." Crescent paced back and forth waving his hands. Good, he was distracted with an evil villain monologue... Perfect. "We need a strong leader to take over in Volkov's absence. Someone who can help the wolves come out of the darkness and be stronger than ever. That's what Mikhail wanted, wasn't it?"

Holy fuck. Niko glared at Crescent. "You don't know anything about what Mik wanted. Don't think for a second you could be half the Tzar he was and would have been for our kind. He was a good man and could have..."

He held back the wave of nausea, but only barely. Mik had wanted to change the world, to lead the wolves out of the old ways. It was Niko's fault he would never be able to.

"Yes." The bastard stopped pacing and stared right into Niko's soul. "Well, he can't, can he? Because you murdered him. It's time someone took over and ended the chaos before the infighting destroys us all. Since you won't step up, I will."

It was damn hard to not walk up to this ignorant manipulator and punch him in the face for even daring to think he could be half the Tzar Mikhail had been. Niko clenched his fists and gritted his teeth. "You wouldn't know progress if it bit you in the ass. You wanted to marry your daughter off to my brother to create an alliance. That is the opposite of what Mik had in mind for our future. We aren't in the dark ages."

"No, we aren't." Crescent folded his arms across his chest. "It's time for wolves to come out of the dark and take our rightful place."

Shit... Niko should have known. "You're a fucking one-blood."

"Don't be stupid, boy. The one-bloods are nothing more than trailer trash who can't think for themselves. They'll support me because I know how to say what they want to hear." A couple of the wolves who were surrounding them paused in their incessant growling and looked quizzically at their alpha. That was news to some of them, and they weren't all happy about it. Crescent either didn't notice or didn't care. "No, son, I'm not a one-blood. They have never thought big enough, can't see beyond their own greed. I'm going to make wolfkind great again, and you're going to help me."

"What do you want?" Because Niko would do everything in his power to do the opposite.

"We'll start with Tzar of the Wolves. That's all you need to know for now."

"Afraid I can't help you with that." Stupid bigoted jackass. "There is no Tzar anymore. The Volkovs' reign is over. It's time to make a new way in the world."

"Just because your little fuckbuddy is dead, doesn't mean

the Volkovs won't put another Tzar on the throne. They're just waiting for the right wolf to step up and show himself."

Rage swelled behind Niko's breastbone, burning through the walls he'd put up around the wounds to his heart and soul when Mik died. No one would denigrate Mikhail Volkov. "Watch what you say, Crescent."

"Or what? You'll kill me too?"

Fucking hell. Niko couldn't do a damn thing about Ramsey Crescent's vile mouth, and he'd let the bastard get to him. This whole damn time he should have been focusing on getting Zara to safety, not allowing himself to be riled up about a past he couldn't change.

He took a deep breath and forced himself to back down. Now was not the time to get killed. He reached out for Zara again. She was still there and probably freaked out as fuck. He couldn't scent her fear, but he could hear that her breathing was steady and normal. Maybe she was stronger than he thought. Good. At least one of them was.

Crescent laughed. "No. I didn't think so. Not in front of your girlfriend. You can't stand for her to see what you really are, can you?"

"I'm losing patience with your evil plans to take over the world. Tell me what it is you want from me." So, he could steal this stupid car and relay all of this to Max and Kosta. Who could actually do something about this invasion?

Crescent rolled his neck, stretching as if this were a casual chat over biscuits and tea. "There are only two ways to become Tzar. Get support from enough packs that the Volkovs are forced to appoint the people's choice or face rebellion."

Niko ran his hand along the edge of the car again hoping

to run into Zara's fingers so she would be ready to make their move. "Yeah, good luck with that. The Troikas will never back you, and without our support, you lose that popularity vote."

"Or an alpha's challenge."

What a dumbass. "It's a little hard to challenge the Tzar when there isn't one."

"Ah, but I could challenge the alpha who killed the Tzar. The only wolf who has a rightful claim to the throne. Now, who could that be?"

Niko stumbled back and had to steady himself against the hood of the car beside them. "My brother has taken over the pack. I'm not an alpha."

"Oh, I think we all know you are. Your father made it no secret that he bred three alphas. Your mother always worried about how she'd keep you boys from tearing each other's heads off when you got older. Why do you suppose they sent you to Russia in the first place?"

He did know. It was the only way his father had talked Niko into leaving Rogue, leaving Zara. If he'd stayed, he and his brothers wouldn't be able to suppress their inner alpha's and the inherent need for control of the pack. The marriage contract for Max with Taryn Crescent was so that his brother could inherit a pack of his own someday. His mother was working tirelessly to find a similar match for Kosta.

Or that's what Piotr Troika had told Niko. He'd warned him that when both Max and Kosta came of age Niko would want to kill them both.

"I don't need a seer to tell that you realize the truth of what I say, Troika. I'm sure your wolf's compulsion to be the alpha is half of what led you to challenge and kill Mikhail in the first place. But you're too weak to rule all of wolfkind.

Your pretty little mama ensured that with her crusade for our kind to mate whomever we want." The enforcers surrounding them made yips that were equivalent to derisive chuckles.

Ramsey Crescent may not believe he was a one-blood, but his ideals ticked all the right boxes. Only he was worse. He didn't just want wolves to take a superior place over humans, spouting the vitriol, he'd taken action. The knowledge that no matter what Niko did or wanted to do, Crescent had the upper hand, curdled in his stomach.

Niko couldn't do a damn thing to stop him. He might be able to save Zara from having to live under Crescent's thumb though. "You want an alpha's challenge against me to claim the throne of Tzar of the Wolves?"

"Yes," Crescent hissed.

"I accept."

"No, Niko. What are you doing?" Zara whispered under her breath. "This is a bad idea."

Crescent's eyes glowed, his wolf pushing near the surface and coming out to play. In another second, he'd shift and both of them would be dead in an instant.

"With conditions." If he was going to die, he'd make sure he was the only one.

His opponent growled. "What conditions?"

"Whether you win or lose the challenge, you never see, touch, or even scent Zara again. You will leave her and her family alone forever." Niko might not have his wolf anymore, but he was surprised to discover he still had his alpha voice. Its power rang through his words making Crescent cringe.

"I don't have to agree to shit terms like that." He swiped his hand through the air. "A seer would be very helpful to me when I'm Tzar. No."

"Then there will be no challenge." And he and Zara were going to have to run for their lives.

Zara stepped between the two of them, her eyes glowing with a bright white light. "The challenge will take place on the eve of the new moon. Only then will the Tzar take his rightful place upon claiming the woman before you as his true mate. All of wolfkind will bow to his reign."

DENIAL AIN'T A RIVER, SISTER

*D*og gone it, why couldn't she hold it together for a few more minutes? Niko was about to get the two of them out of this nightmare. Her mind was already playing tricks on her. Every other word she heard was wolf, or pack, or wolf pack. She wasn't even following what they were saying anymore.

When Ramsey Crescent appeared, she wanted nothing more than to stab him in the eyeball with the pen in her pocket. It was filled with red ink, and she'd get so much joy seeing his blood mix with the color of correction. If that made her truly insane, then so be it.

Then all the other wolves... or whatever they were in reality, poodles or hamsters or cockroaches for all she knew, had popped up, surrounding them. Niko wasn't freaking out that a bunch of drooling wolves were snarling at them, so they must not be there. When she looked at their glowing red eyes, she couldn't tell if they were wolves or men. They were both at the same time.

Okay. They must be Crescent's lackeys, which were

similar to cockroaches. They were outnumbered, so now was not the time to get away with killing their leader. Besides if she took him out here in the middle of the street, she might not find out the status of the other women, and she certainly wouldn't be able to save them.

Zara needed to be more deliberate with her plans to take the Crescent crew out and rescue those he still held captive. She'd almost made the mistake of acting irrationally, which would not only have gotten her dead, but Niko too.

He didn't deserve that.

She gripped the handle of the car door tight in her hand, trying to listen, praying she'd catch Niko's signal to yank it open and jump inside. It was the only thing grounding her. The blood was pumping through her ears so loudly. She took slow yoga breaths just to keep from screaming at them both to shut up and leave her alone.

"You want an alpha's challenge against me to claim the throne of Tzar of the Wolves?" Niko's voice changed into something she'd heard before but didn't want to admit to herself when or where.

"Yes," Crescent hissed like the snake he was.

"I accept."

"No, Niko. What are you doing?" Zara whispered under her breath. She didn't understand what he was agreeing to, but she knew deep down from her toes to her nose that he was in danger. "This is a bad idea."

Crescent's eyes glowed. No, no, no. The hallucination was taking full hold. Soon she wouldn't know what was happening around her at all. Please, no. She tried breathing in through her nostrils and out through her mouth. She reached for Niko, but he'd stepped away from her.

She needed him. He grounded her, not the stupid car.

"With conditions." She heard Niko talking, but through a fog.

His opponent growled. "What conditions?"

"Whether you win or lose the challenge, you never see, touch, or even scent Zara again. You will leave her and her family alone forever." Niko's voice rang with power, and it almost pulled her back to reality.

"I don't have to mah mah mah maaaah maaah mah mahh maaaaaah." Crescents words faded into incoherence.

Zara's vision tunneled and tingles raced across her skin. The vision was going to hit hard.

Niko spoke again, and Zara couldn't breathe, couldn't see anything but white light. If she didn't know better, she'd think she was dead.

Don't go into the light. Like she was going to heaven anyway. Not with the plans for murder in her heart. Well, if she went to hell, at least she wanted to commit the actual crime that would send her there. At the moment that wasn't looking likely.

Great. Now Niko knew for sure she was not normal. That would be the end of that relationship... Fine... Whatever. It wasn't going anywhere anyway. Or if it was, she would have to put a stop to it before she led Niko down the path of destruction with her.

Once again, her brain was being a dickhead. Her body moved of its own accord and words came out of her mouth. None of which she had any control over. She only barely understood the sounds coming out in her own voice. Something about a challenge and a claim and a mate.

The scene in front of her was clear as a quiet morning after a snowstorm.

Her skin throbbed, but in a warm and comforting way. Niko towered over her from behind, one hand in her hair, holding her tight. A flutter moved through her chest and down, down, down, settling in her lower belly. Her mouth watered, and she licked her lips. She longed to touch him, but her hands and arms wouldn't move.

They were tied to a wooden chair in front of her. With red rope looped in a gorgeously intricate knot.

"Your soft luscious ass takes the paddle so well, *solnyshka*. Shall we see if your spanking made you wet and ready for me?"

"Yes, please." Was that her voice, husky and trembling with need?

"Good girl." His hand skating across her sensitive skin, barely touching her, making the glow of her hot flesh prickle and tingle.

Zara whimpered, not wanting him to tease her anymore. She needed him. Needed him to take her, make her come, make her his. "Please, Niko."

"Are you sure? I won't be gentle with your body this time. I will take you hard, make you come on my cock, make your body and mind mine."

She swallowed past the need choking her and nodded, so ready for him.

He touched his lips to her ear and whispered darkly, "Say it, Zarenity. Say you want to be mine. Say you want me to make you mine."

"I'm already yours, Niko. I–"

Niko growled low and pushed her head to the side. He

licked the skin between her throat and her shoulder, sending spikes of pleasure through her so sharp she almost came on the spot. She held back knowing he wouldn't want that, but she wouldn't be able to for much longer.

His lick turned into a scrape of his teeth and then–

Niko's voice called to her, but it wasn't filled with lust and desire, but instead fear. "Zara? Zara? *Solnyshka*, sweetheart, can you hear me?"

Zara blinked and shook her head. "Niko?"

"Thank the Goddess. I thought you..." He squeezed her to his chest so tight she could barely breathe. But in a good way. It was nice being so close to him. But breathing was nice too.

"Nee Koh. Can't. Breathe."

"Sorry... Sorry." He released her from the tight hold he had on her, but he kept her in his arms.

"Niko, dear. If you don't let her go, Doc won't be able to look at her and make sure she's okay." Selena's voice filtered through and Zara turned thirty-one flavors of blushing.

All Zara could see was Niko's t-shirt in front of her eyes, but if his mom and the town vet were here, there was a good chance a whole slew of other people were too. Which meant they weren't in the street by her house anymore, and they'd all been witness to her having a very naughty fantasy about Niko.

She buried her face in his chest willing her cheeks to return back to a normal shade before she had to deal with anyone. Maybe Niko was the only one who'd seen her mentally break into a million pieces. She peeked an eye open.

Nope. Her sister was here along with her boyfriend, and Gal, and Max, and Selena and Doc. Hail, hail, the gang's all here. Great. Just great. They were probably going to want to send her to the hospital again. Before she tucked her face back into her hiding place, she glanced around to make sure they weren't already on the psych ward.

Plush, expensive furniture, a piano, and a tasteful chandelier. Definitely not the loony bin. It had changed a little since she'd been here in high school, but she'd never forget Niko's parents' front room. He'd brought her home.

"Zara, is it okay if I check you over? You were out for longer than I'd expect. I won't touch you if you don't want me to, but I'd like to test your pupils." Doc's voice was always so calm and collected. That's probably what made him great in emergencies.

She wasn't sure what a veterinarian would understand mental disorders in humans, but what did she know? She'd gone to law school. Maybe cats and dogs and parakeets suffered from maladies of the brain too.

Doc approached slowly and pulled out a small pen light. She did her best to keep her eyes wide and blank, but ended up blinking more than usual. He finished with her pupil check and while she waited for the spots to fade, he looked the rest of her over, keeping his promise not to touch. "When you were...gone, did anyone...bite you?"

"What? No." Something niggled in the back of Zara's mind. A memory, or the snippet of one?

Doc nodded, and Selena took his place. "*Lapochka*, what did you see?"

Blush. Selena was a cool mom and all, but there was no way she was telling anyone about the very naughty fantasy she'd had.

"Zara?"

"I don't know what you mean." If she didn't go to hell for contemplating murder, she would for how many lies she told.

Selena didn't let up. "In your vision. Did you see who becomes the Tzar?"

No visions here. Not a single one. No hallucinations or fantasies either. Time to deflect. "Of Russia? They have an elected government now, right? Is Putin trying to become Tzar? Doesn't he have enough power? I don't watch much news these days."

Selena tapped her fingers on her leg and then leaned forward. "No, dear, not of Russia. The Tzar of Wolfkind."

Wolfkind. She said it like mankind or humankind. Zara's throat went thick, and she wanted to scratch and claw at it. Wolfkind wasn't a thing. Not in real life. Only in her visions. Only in her mind. Her very broken mind.

The whole place got silent as if they were all waiting for her to laugh hysterically and start flinging her own poo at them.

Niko stood and took Zara's hand, pulling her to her feet. "I think Zara's had enough for tonight. She needs to rest."

Several voices rose up in protest, but he gave the room a death stare, and they all went quiet. That was fine by her. Niko wasn't wrong. She was exhausted. "Can you take me home now?"

"No, you're staying here, and I'm not letting you out of my sight." He dragged her from the fancy front room and toward where she knew the family's bedrooms were. "Crescent may be a power-hungry grandstander, but he wouldn't dare invade the Troika pack house. You'll be safe here."

Zara frowned at his phrasing, but she followed him down the hall to his bedroom. The same one he'd had in high school.

With the bed where she'd lost her virginity. He thought that was safe? Safe for who?

Niko finally let her go and shut the door behind them. He took a deep breath and placed a hand flat on the wood, bowing his head, not looking at her. Zara already didn't like where this was going. Niko had never been nervous to talk to her before. Whatever he was trying to work up his nerve to say wouldn't be good.

Still facing the door, he said, "*Solnyshka*, I understand you don't remember much about your kidnapping, but I know you recognized Ramsey Crescent tonight."

See, not good. She wouldn't to deny she knew who that bastard was. She never could lie to Niko. "That man is a beast and needs to be stopped."

He turned, and his face reflected exactly how angry she was inside. He looked almost scary. "I agree with both of those things, but he's a different kind than you think. Those wolves you saw tonight, they weren't simply trained animals."

That she wouldn't admit to. Nope. No. No way. Why would he even say that? "I didn't see any wolves."

"It's okay. You did see them, and they weren't just wolves. They were... I am... was..." Niko stalked closer to her and Zara backed away. "Fuck. I - I don't want to scare you."

She bumped into a wooden chair. One that looked way too familiar. She swallowed and took another step away. "You already are."

Niko held out his hands, palms up. "I promise you are always safe with me. I would never do anything to hurt you. In fact, I can't."

Oh, he could definitely hurt her. He already had. It had

taken a long time to recover from a broken heart. She wasn't entirely sure she ever had. "Can't what?"

"Never mind. There are things I think you already understand, but your head is playing tricks on you because it's too unbelievable."

Oh God. If he only knew. Wait. Did he have her all figured out?

"I promise what I'm about to tell you isn't a joke, and if you search your memories, you know that werewolves are real. The Crescents are wolf shifters, yes, but so is my family. My parents, Max, Kosta, a good third of the residents of Rogue too. We aren't monsters like in the movies, we just have an ability humans don't."

Zara's heart and lungs turned to rock and spots danced in front of her eyes. She wanted to yell and scream that he was trying to deceive her, that he was wrong, but she couldn't. Not because her limbs and jaw and throat didn't work.

Because she knew he wasn't lying. She knew.

Werewolves were real.

She'd been kidnapped by them.

A sudden chill gripped her. So cold. When she finally took a breath again, her muscles rebelled against the intake of oxygen to her blood, and her legs went out from under her.

Niko caught her and lifted her up like a swooning princess. He carried her to his bed and carefully set her down. "It's okay, *solnyshka*. Everything is going to be okay. I won't let anyone hurt you. You're safe."

Her teeth clacked and chattered, and her whole body trembled. Zara wrapped her arms around herself and rubbed fast and hard across her skin to warm herself back up, but nothing was working.

Niko ripped the blankets away, sat on the bed, pulled her into him, and covered them both up. "Shh, shh, shh. I've got you. You're safe, Zara. Shh, don't cry, baby."

Until he said it, she didn't realize tears were running down her face. She laid her head on his shoulder and let the sobs take over.

Those bastards had taken her, right from her own home. They'd thrown her into an isolated room afraid and alone, and they'd terrorized her with what she'd thought were horrific visions of monsters. But it had all been real. Every fucking moment.

She cried for the life that had been taken away from her, cried for the years of worry that she was batshit crazy, cried for the woman she'd wanted to become and hadn't out of fear. Zara sobbed until there were no more tears. Slowly, she let her memories sort themselves out, and, while she didn't understand everything, she thought that, at least from the past month, she knew the difference between reality and what her mind was trying to protect her from.

It was all real.

All of it.

Which meant her mission to take down Ramsey Crescent and save those women was even more imperative than ever before. She was not going to let that man, wolf, whatever he was, hurt anyone else for his own self-interest. That included Niko.

He crooned sweet nothings to her, and rocked her in the warmth of his arms, until she finally quieted. They stayed like that for a long time, until dawn's early rays poked through his window shades.

"Niko?"

"Yeah?"

"You can't go to that challenge." She had a really bad feeling about what would happen if he did.

Niko held her tighter and tucked his chin into the crook of her neck just like he used to all those years ago. "I don't have a choice. Even if I hadn't already accepted the challenge, this is the best way for me to serve my family and to keep you safe."

"What if I ask you not to go?" Not that it had worked before.

He straightened up and turned her chin, so she had to look at him. "Did you see something in your vision that you don't want to tell me?"

"Yes, but not about any of that." Being wrapped up in Niko's arms, in his bed, with that damn chair staring at her for the past few hours, that dirty scene had played in her head a few too many times. It had felt all too real, and she didn't want to admit that she wanted every little bit of what she'd seen to happen.

He raised one knowing eyebrow. "Can we talk about that instead?"

Zara tore her chin from his warmth and looked as far away as possible. "I don't think so. I'm trying to understand what this whole vision thing means. I've been having them for so long, and I thought I was crazy. Like literally. I'm still not sure that I'm not."

"How long?"

She wasn't ready to answer that. "What if I go with you to the challenge? You've already made the condition that he can't touch me either way. Will he honor that?"

Even if he didn't, she had some planning to do, and a

whole lot of questions for Galyna and Heli about what killed werewolves. It couldn't be as easy as a silver bullet.

A rumble came from Niko's chest that sounded an awful lot like a growl. Except this one didn't scare her. She liked it. Weirdo.

"You're not going."

How could she explain this so he'd understand? "Niko. You've always been strong and confident, so I don't expect you to comprehend how devastating having all of my own power taken away from me has been. I need to find a way to take it back."

"I get it, *solnyshka*. Much more than you think."

The way he said that, something about the sad dark tone of his voice made her think of the white wolf and bloody snow.

SACRIFICIAL WOLF

*N*iko sat at the end of the bar nursing a beer. Yes, he was having beer for breakfast. While his brothers were freaking out at him, he might as well relax, because they weren't going to change his mind.

Max hadn't stopped pacing since Niko had told him about Ramsey Crescent's plans. "You should have talked to me before you agreed to something so fucking stupid."

"Or me." Kosta tried not to look pissed off by leaning against the bar all nonchalantly, but he couldn't hide the glower on his face and the purple glow rimming his eyes as his wolf hovered near the surface.

He did love his brothers for trying to protect him. They were both alphas of their own packs now, and he'd expect no less. But Niko wasn't one of their wolves. He belonged to no pack, even if Max claimed him as a Troika. It was the only reason he hadn't become a lone wolf when he'd mysteriously been brought back to America.

He didn't want to hurt his family. Making the decision to go through with this challenge was the first time he felt like he was doing something for them instead of being the cause of all their troubles.

"There wasn't time to check in with my little brothers when Zara and I were surrounded by half the Crescent Bay Pack's Enforcers. I had to make a decision then and there and I'm sticking to it." Niko took a long sip of his beer and stared at Max. They both knew he was accusing Max of not protecting his territory without saying it outright. That was his job as a big brother, to poke at his siblings' bruises.

Max didn't much like getting his wounds prodded. Never had.

"Dammit, Niko. I could put a stop to this. I'm your alpha." Max brought his alpha voice out for that last bit, the voice that any pack member had no choice but to obey. He hadn't given Niko a direct order with it, so he'd used it for show.

Unfortunately for them both, it was the wrong channel. Once their father had died, no alpha voice but that of the Tzar would ever have that effect on Niko ever again.

Niko took a long slug, finishing his drink in a couple of gulps, and set the glass down on the bar carefully so as not to break it. He looked straight ahead and not at his brother. "We both know that you're not."

"What, you're challenging me now? You want to take the Troika pack back from me?" Max growled and his wolf's eyes burned with the Troika blue fire in his soul. "Let's see you try."

Sigh. Niko deserved that. He'd gotten an alpha's hackles up, what did he expect? He should show his brother some respect, but something deep inside of him wouldn't back down. Not enough to allow Max to have any real power over him. That was Mik's fault. Mik had shown Niko exactly how to bring the dominant out in himself, and he'd never been able to be anything else ever since.

Niko would never challenge his brother's authority, not really. Especially since he'd lost his wolf somewhere deep inside. He didn't know if he'd ever be able to get the ability to shift back or if the Goddess had forsaken him for what he'd done. But he still couldn't let his brother make decisions for him. "I will never be the alpha I was meant to be, brother. You're a good leader, and I wouldn't be doing my job if I didn't get you a bit riled up every once in a while. I get paid extra for that you know."

His words and tone were light and playful, to deflect the only men in the world who might be able to see the darkness in his soul for what it truly was. They couldn't save him. The encounter with Crescent had shown Niko he couldn't save himself by trying to live as a human either.

He could save them though, from Ramsey Crescent and his one-blood ideals. He would sacrifice himself for that. He didn't know how he would kill Crescent yet, because it wasn't with his own wolf in a fair challenge. He would eliminate the bastard and probably go down trying.

He would destroy Crescent for deigning to think he could fill the shoes of Mik, someone as compassionate, smart, and who genuinely wanted to help his people as the Tzar of the Wolves. But most especially, Niko would end Ramsey Crescent for making Zara cry.

She was his one regret in this plan. If he'd figured his shit out sooner, he wouldn't have tried to get close to her again. She was going to be so pissed when she found out he was leaving her again and this time, never coming back. He'd be lucky if she didn't Ouija board his ass back from the afterlife just to rail at him.

She was also the only reason he'd called his brothers to meet him before he headed to Cape Cod where the Crescent compound loomed. He needed to make arrangements for Zara and warn his brothers of the trouble that would come should he fail to kill Ramsey Crescent.

He wouldn't fail. He would use his own weakness to draw Crescent in. A challenge was meant to be wolf against wolf, to the death. The winner's prize was void and taking over a pack as alpha was forfeit, if either combatant cheated by using any other weapon besides their own teeth, claws, and cunning.

It didn't matter to Niko. He would kill Crescent by any means necessary.

He'd figure out exactly what those means were going to be later. Traditional weapons certainly wouldn't work. Wolves would smell the oil and powder of a gun a million miles away. Same went for the metal of knives. What he needed was a good old-fashioned Russian gulag shiv.

"Listen, you aren't going to talk me out of doing the challenge. That's not why I called you in. I'm here to ask you to take care of Zara afterwards. Her prophecy said that the winner of the challenge would claim her as his true mate. Should I fail, you cannot let Ramsey Crescent anywhere near her."

"Niko—" Max's tone alone was already protesting.

"Seriously, Maksim. I know you're already defending our family name and territory in the wake of Mik's death. I'm sorry for that, for the trouble I caused you. This is the first time I've gotten a chance to make up for that, the only chance I have to make any sort of preparations for..."

He still couldn't bring himself to say it out loud.

Kosta slapped him on the back and brought Niko back from the brink of sinking into the cycle of reliving Mik's death over and over in his mind.

"You've been trying to get yourself killed since you got back. We aren't going to let you die, dumbass. Not for your misguided sense of justice or any other reason. You want to go fight Crescent, I say go for it. The asshole has death coming his way from one of us eventually anyway. But let's come up with a real plan, one that all three of us can execute."

Well, shit. That was hard to argue with. "There's something you don't know."

Max shook his head. "There's a lot of things we don't know, but three heads are better than one. We always made a good team. Let's get the band back together and rock 'n roll right over Crescent's fucking face."

If he told them, they weren't going to want him to go at all. They'd work even harder to keep him here. They'd probably usurp his plan out of their misguided need to protect him and end up getting themselves killed. "I need you to understand that what I'm about to tell you makes me the one and only person who can go in and take Crescent out."

"Whatever, dude. Yeah, yeah, yeah. You're the biggest, you're the strongest, you've been trained by the Volkovs. We get it." Kosta rolled his eyes prepared for a speech Niko wasn't going to give him.

"No, I have no doubt at this point, both of you are stronger, faster, more deadly wolves than I am." Niko held up a hand when Max tried to interrupt. He wished he hadn't finished his drink because his mouth was dry. "I'm the only one who can do this, because I can be sacrificed. Neither of you can."

"Shut the fuck up." Max rubbed his forehead like Niko was giving him a headache. "Nobody is going to be sacrificed. Get off your martyr high-horse and get back in the game, man. "

A headache was the least of his brothers' worries if they tried to engage with Crescent. He was an older, wiser, more experienced alpha than anyone else on this side of the Atlantic. Their father would have been the only other wolf that could have bested him in a challenge and that would have only been a fifty-fifty shot. No. Niko had to do this. "You two have to protect your packs, your mates, and our society. You understand better than anyone else the future Mik wanted for wolfkind."

"We know what mom's told us. You're the one who was friends with him. If anyone knew what he wanted, it was you. You should be the next Tzar, Niko." Kosta hadn't entirely lost the hero worship he'd had for Niko as a kid.

He would soon enough. Niko hated that he was going to let them down. Because he would never be Tzar. Never. "I can't."

Max put his hand on Niko's shoulder, a gesture meant to be comforting that somehow only made Niko feel more alone. "I know Mik's death was hard on you and I hope someday you'll tell us what happened, but–"

"No. I. Can't." He took a deep breath. "I've lost my wolf."

"What do you mean?" Kosta scoffed. "You can't just misplace your wolf. It's not like you left it in Russia."

"I can't shift." The words came like angry porcupines coming out of his throat. "I can't even feel that part of myself anymore. The Goddess has forsaken me. I'm not a wolf anymore. I'm no more a wolf, than any other human."

His brothers stood there staring at him with their mouths hanging open for so long that he finally reached over and chucked them both on the chin just to keep the bugs from flying in. Max jerked away and scowled, but Kosta's jaw fell right back open.

"What in the hell makes you think you should go into a challenge with an asshole like Crescent then? You're not going." Max slashed his hand through the air.

"Max, don't you see? I'm expendable, and this is a good shot at taking him out. Once he finds out I can't shift, he'll let his guard down. That's when I'll be able to take him out. We can't allow a one-blood to become the new Tzar." Crescent would not only destroy their world with his ambition, he'd affect the human population too.

"What about Zara's premonition?" Kosta asked. "If you kill Crescent, you'll have to finally claim her. We all already know she's your true mate."

Niko swiped at the back of his neck, wiping away the chilled sweat pooling along his hairline.

"What do you mean everybody knows? Maybe Crescent is her fated mate. Just because we dated in high school, doesn't mean shit." Which was a lie straight from the pits of hell. Niko had always known she was it for him, forever. But if he didn't claim her then she would be free to live a normal life.

Max looked like he was about done with Niko. "A. Because you gave her those psychic abilities when you marked her, and B. duh. It's pretty damned obvious."

"Back up. Gave her psychic abilities? What the fuck are you talking about?"

Kosta got right up in his face. "Did you or did you not bite Zara?"

"What the hell? Were you some horny-ass pre-teen watching us having sex? That's plain fucking weird, even for you, Kosta."

"Oh my God, you don't know." Kosta shook his head wide-eyed. "You've been living under a rock since you got back. I thought the Volkovs would have told you, or at least Mik. Sneaky secretive bastards."

Niko didn't have psychic abilities like Zara seemed to, but his spidey-senses were tingling. "Know what? That you were a disgusting peeping-Tom as a kid? Does Heli know?"

Max snorted at Kosta, but took over. "The bite, dickhead. That's why the Volkovs forbid us to bite humans and made it taboo so long ago. Our bite either turns our mates into a wolf-shifter themselves or gives them psychic abilities. Gal's wolf is fucking gorgeous, and Heli's psychic ability is, uh, strange."

Kosta smacked Max in the back of the head. "Zara said none of the Crescents bit her, ergo, you did. Although, I wondered because she doesn't have a mark on her neck or shoulder that I could see."

It was Niko's turn for his jaw to drop, like down past his chin, all the way to the floor. "That's because it's not on her neck."

"Where is it?" they asked in unison.

That was for Niko to know and his brothers never to find out. Because if either of them ever got a glimpse of the creamy soft skin on Zara's inner thigh, he was going to have to hang them from a tall tree by their dicks.

"I need to go see her." Zara thought she'd been going crazy

for years, and it was his fault. What exactly would he say to her when he saw her again? Sorry for causing your mental breakdown? Shit. Maybe he shouldn't say anything at all. What good would it do?

"Good, so you're not going up to Crescent Bay?" Max asked.

Niko pushed away from the bar and stood up, facing away from his brothers. "I didn't say that."

Now more than ever, he had to pay for his sins.

Kosta, like the exuberant pup turned angry wolf he was, stepped right in Niko's way and gave him a shove back toward his seat. "You'll resign Zara to a miserable, loveless existence?"

He was doing this for her. "She doesn't need me. I've already ruined her life a couple of times over. She'll find someone else. Plenty of people do just fine without a true mate. Look at mom."

Max joined Kosta, blocking Niko from moving toward the door, toward his one chance to do the right thing for them all. When had his little brothers gotten so big and fierce? "For being so smart, you're awfully fucking dumb. Mom started an entire revolution so we could be with our soulmates. She wanted better for us. I hope someday she can find her true mate too, because it certainly wasn't dad."

All the more reason for Niko to ensure the one-bloods didn't rule. His own life was already doomed. He had to believe Zara would be able to find love again. She deserved far better than him.

"I want what's best for mom and Zara." The boys could easily block his way. They were wolf-shifters, Alphas, and were raised to protect those weaker than them, especially pack. He doubted he could ever make them understand what he had to do.

Niko set a hand on each of their shoulders, knowing he couldn't lie to them, he couldn't trick them, he could only persuade them with the last tool he had in his arsenal. He wasn't sure until last night he still had access to it, but something about being near Zara, needing to protect her had brought his alpha voice back. He put the power of it into his words, knowing they would hate him for it, but that they would have to obey. "Let me go, brothers."

Max and Kosta bowed their heads under the compulsion of the alpha, though their wolves shimmered in the glow of their eyes. If Niko lived through the coming days, there would be hell to pay.

If he died, that hell would come a whole lot sooner.

I SEE DEAD PEOPLE

*Z*ara slept and slept, like she hadn't closed her eyes in a million years. She knew exactly when Niko got out of bed, but she couldn't pull herself out of that exhaustion to wake up.

The sun sparkled through the window when they'd finally fallen asleep, but now as she peeled one of her eyes open, the light came from a different angle. She'd slept the whole day. Actually, for all she knew, she could have been unconscious for several days. Except Niko hadn't returned, so she didn't think she'd been out for two whole nights.

She found her way to his bathroom, peed, washed her face, and couldn't quite talk herself into using his toothbrush. Her finger and some toothpaste would have to do. She avoided looking at herself in the mirror. She wasn't ready for that shitshow.

Women's voices drifted down the hallway, and she thought she smelled coffee and something sweet and baked. Heli's chocolate croissants would help anyone make it through a rough morning, or evening as the case may be. She followed her ears and nose to the kitchen and took two deep breaths before entering.

She needed just one more second to pull herself together and then she could face the women. They'd seen her at her worst last night, or however long ago it had been, and it was going to take some work to repair her fall from grace in their eyes.

Selena spotted her first, but kept quiet, simply waited for her to do her thing. Heli and Gal were there too, as she knew they would be, and one more woman Zara didn't recognize. Even more reason to put that I'm-Okay-You're-Okay armor back on.

Show time. "I'd kill for one of those croissants and some coffee if you have it."

"Done and done." Selena smiled and got up to grab Zara a mug. "But we also have wine if you'd like."

"Coffee first, with lots of cream and sugar." She preferred a little caffeine with her sweet creamer. Zara sat down in the empty chair between Gal and Heli.

Gal took her hand and gave it a squeeze, but Heli didn't look at her at all. She swirled a chocolate covered cookie in her glass of wine. That wasn't a good sign.

Gal must have sensed the tension between the sisters because she cleared her throat and motioned toward the other woman sitting at the table with them. "Zara, this is Violet. She's a part of Heli's... umm, well, her pack."

Violet gave a little wave but didn't say anything. She glanced at Heli, seeming to be taking her cue from her. Smart lady. Zara had suffered enough of her younger sister's upsets to know it was best to wait it out. Eventually, Heli would spout out what was on her mind. Either that or push at

Zara's buttons until they both boiled over and had a big ole fight.

"Here's your coffee." Selena handed her a steaming mug that had not just a coffee aroma, but an herblike aroma too. "I put a little something special in it."

It smelled divine. "What is it?"

"A concoction Doc gave me. It's good for you, I promise. Drink up, it will help you feel a thousand times better than what any regular cup of java can do for you."

Bottoms up then, because Zara could use all the help she could get.

"Why didn't you tell me." Heli's voice had that quality of both disappointment and hurt that Zara had worked to avoid their entire lives. "Niko said it's been going on for years.

She wouldn't deflect or pretend she didn't understand what her sister was asking. She'd hidden a lot from Heli but had never outright lied to her. "I didn't want to burden you with my problems."

"You don't always have to protect everyone from everything, you know? It might have been nice for me to have someone to talk to about how weird it is to get visions of the future as well. If you'd told me, maybe I wouldn't have felt so crazy when it started happening to me too."

Zara swallowed her coffee all wrong, and she coughed hard to get the hot burn out of her lungs. Gal patted her on the back, but Heli just sat back in her chair and watched, a muscle ticking in her jaw the whole time.

"You have visions?" Zara croaked out as soon as she got her lungs working right.

Heli leaned in close and whispered, "I see dead people."

Gulp.

"I'm kidding." She chuckled and leaned forward, reengaged, the anger gone. "I've always wanted to say that. But, yeah. Ever since Kosta marked and claimed me, I get teensy tiny glimpses into the future. Like I saw that you were gonna try to breathe your coffee."

Marked? Claimed? "Sorry, reverse, start over. What? Kosta did what now?"

"Funny that you struggled with that part and not the bit about how I can see the future." Heli rolled her eyes and took a sip of her wine.

From what little she trusted of her own memory, Zara understood about wolf shifters mating. Crescent had gone on and on about getting his daughter Taryn mated to a powerful wolf. He'd made it perfectly clear that he wouldn't allow any of his pack to mate a human. But he didn't mind the men screwing around with any women they wanted. Bastard.

Was marking and claiming what wolves did when they wanted to dick around with a human? Crap. Was that what Kosta and Max had done to Heli and Gal? She was going to kill all three of the Troika brothers if that was the case.

The other woman, Violet, watched Zara warily and continued to keep her mouth shut. She understood what Heli was saying though. She had a wariness in her eyes and held her mug against her chest like it was armor. "If you don't know what any of this means, you might want to switch over to that wine now."

Eek. Zara picked up Heli's glass and downed it in two gulps. "I'm ready."

"It's like this." Gal had that look when she was about to either teach a master's level course on some arcane bit of trivia or had really juicy gossip. Thank goodness she was going to come to Zara's rescue with the offer of information like the smart librarian that she was. "We'd better start at the beginning. When wolf shifters such as Max, Kosta, and Niko find their true mate, they are driven by instinct to mark and claim them so other wolves know not to try any funny business. Then under the full moon in a, uhh, ahem, special ritual, the two are mated. When a wolf marks his or her mate with a bite, interesting things happen if that mate isn't a wolf-shifter. Some develop magical or psychic abilities, and some get the ability to shift."

Gal exchanged a look with Selena who nodded. They both stood and each whipped off their tops.

"Whoa. Uh, that was unexpected. Do we all have to get naked for this part of the explanation?" Because that would be weird.

"They don't want to ruin their nice clothes. Think about it." Heli softly prodded, not so angry now.

Zara didn't want the unbidden, memories of men and women in the Crescent compound walking around naked like it was no biggie popped into her brain. Eww.

Gal pointed to the place between her shoulder and neck that bore a gorgeous looking tattoo of a blue moon, with bite marks along the edges, and a black wolf in the center. That kind of ink didn't really fit Galyna's cute kids' librarian vibe. "This is my mark, from Max. Heli and Violet have them as well. I suspect you do too."

Zara squirmed in her seat and it took a lot of effort not to cross her legs or put her hand over her inner thigh. "I don't have any tattoos."

That wasn't a lie. Zara had never had a tattoo artist or

their needles and ink anywhere near her skin. As far as she knew.

Heli yanked the collar of her t-shirt to the side and revealed a design similar to the one on Gal's shoulder. "Yeah, I don't either, but this isn't a tattoo. It's the mark our mates gave to us when they claimed us as theirs."

Zara leaned forward to study the image on her sister's neck. Heli's moon was purple and her wolf was gray. In front of Zara's gaze, the beast moved its head and looked right at her with purple glowing eyes.

Zara jumped back. "That is some freaky Harry Potter level shit, Heli."

Her sister touched the spot and gently rubbed over it in a slow circle. "It's a way that Kosta connects with me when he's feeling especially emotional about something. I'll check in with him in a minute."

"Huh. I wonder if Max can do that too or if that's particular to your gift," Gal said. "See, Zara, this is all new to us too. Max had no idea I'd get a mark or develop an ability because it's been taboo for so long to bite a human. Wolves and humans haven't been allowed to mate since the dark ages and there isn't exactly a beginner's guide to fated mates or anything."

Heli nodded. "Maybe you should write one. Although, that kind of sounds like a romance novel title."

While Zara had been studying Heli's mark, Gal and Selena had both stripped all the way down. While Zara wasn't ashamed of her curves, she didn't quite have the confidence of these women to hang out bare either. Except they didn't just stand there, something was happening.

Their bodies were changing, contorting, bones cracked,

and fur burst through their skin. Their faces elongated, fangs dropped past their lips, and claws sprouted from their hands.

"Just remember, this is all real. You aren't hallucinating. We're showing you this so you can see it for yourself." Selena's voice changed and went quiet as her mouth transformed into the snout of a canine. In the span of a heartbeat, Zara watched wide-eyed as her friend and the mother of her ex-boyfriend transformed into wolves.

Wolves she recognized.

Flashes of a battle with these animals, Heli, Violet, and even Kosta and Niko skittered through her memories. They'd been fighting against Ramsey Crescent. Zara gasped and blinked back tears at the rush of emotions hitting her. Relief, gratitude, determination, fear.

All in the blink of an eye.

"I remember. That night. You all saved me. I thought it was all a nightmare, but it was real." How many times was she going to have to relive moments she'd convinced herself were hallucinations?

Gal, still as a wolf, carefully walked over and gave Zara's hand a nuzzle. The end of her nose was wet and tickled, but it wasn't unpleasant, and Zara rubbed her finger along the fur and up to the soft spot between Gal's ears.

Heli sat up straight in her chair and looked over at Gal. "Oh. They're here or will be in a second."

"Who?" Zara asked.

Max and Kosta walked into the kitchen before Heli could even answer. That would take some getting used to. "You saw that, in a vision just now?"

"Yup. It comes in handy sometimes. Like in a fight. I'm basically a ninja these days." She reached over and grabbed a mug out of the air, that Kosta purposefully knocked off the table.

Max stood in the doorway and took up a whole lot more room than Zara remembered. It wasn't that he was bigger or broader than the last time she'd seen him. His presence was larger than life, and he hadn't even said a word yet. It reminded her of the first day Niko had walked into her life.

"Babe, you should shift back. We all need to talk, and I don't want Zara to feel excluded because she—"

A voice, Selena's voice, popped into her head. *She's family, she can hear us just fine.*

"Umm. Please tell me if anyone else here heard that." Hearing voices was definitely part of her past crazy-pants business. Zara simply couldn't trust her own brain to know the difference until she had a little more experience sorting out reality.

Heli leaned over and kept her voice low, even though Zara had a feeling everyone could hear anyway. "That was Selena in your head. It's a wolf thing. Which proves my point once again that Niko marked you and that's why you've had visions for, what, like eight years, I'm guessing. But I'm also right, aren't I?"

"Shush your face." That was the problem with sisters. They knew too much.

Now that she understood where the image of a wolf silhouette against the moon came from and what it meant, she visualized exactly the moment Niko had marked her. The same night he'd proposed to her. The night before they'd broken up.

She hadn't noticed the image for several days after Niko had left for Russia. She'd scrubbed at it in the bathtub hoping it was just pen and ink. That had been the first time she'd questioned her own sanity, because there was no way she'd purposefully gotten a tattoo on her inner thigh that close to her mons. Then there was the weird fact that she didn't remember going to a shop or an artist.

So many things that she'd chalked up to insanity were making sense now. For about a half a second she wanted to rail at Niko for doing this to her. But for once in eight long years, she was thinking clearly and trusted her own thoughts and logic.

Niko had no idea he had any part in this. He hadn't done it purposefully, anyway. As much as she had hurt feelings over the way they'd broken up, she would never believe he wouldn't have told her that he'd changed her life irrevocably. He wouldn't have left her alone if he'd known they were fated to be mates.

Apparently, fate could go screw itself, because that part hadn't worked out.

Could it still? If their lives were connected by all this magical business, they could try again. After she killed Ramsey Crescent.

For the first time, those plans began to include an escape contingency. Crescent needed to die, but maybe Zara's life didn't have to end too.

"So, where's your mark?" Heli cupped her chin in her hand. "Hmm. Someplace you can hide from me. It's on your butt isn't it?"

Oh, my God. Zara would have to ask Niko if his younger brothers were this irritating too. "You're a butt."

Ladies. Let's save this discussion for later, please. Selena's voice inside her head had the distinct mom tone to it.

"Yes, good idea. Zara, I realize you're still recovering, but we need your help." Max waved his hand between himself and Kosta with that we-need-a-lawyer look on his face.

"I'll do whatever I can. Are you getting sued or something? I have to warn you, I'm better with contracts than criminal investigations." Hopefully it wasn't anything big, because she didn't want to delay her plans to get retribution and then see where things went with Niko.

"I wish it were as simple as that. I'm afraid it's much worse, and we're hoping, because of your connection, you can stop him."

Violet stood and Zara recognized the white glowing eyes as if she were looking in a mirror. "One path leads to death and vengeance, the other to the death and the crown. No matter her choice, fate has intervened, the wolf is coming."

Oi. Was that how she sounded? Zara was going to practice her delivery of creepy prophecies, so she didn't sound like Aughra from the Dark Crystal. "What does that mean?"

Everyone stared at Violet, but when she blinked and looked at them all wide-eyed, it was clear she had no idea what she'd said or seen. Okay then. Zara was the only one who had any experience with this bullshit, and she was smart enough to figure it out. "Max, what were you about to say right before Violet went all crystal ball on us?"

"I don't like where this is going. Niko has gone to fight Ramsey Crescent in an alpha challenge and commanded us to let him go."

He used his alpha voice on you, didn't he?

Max and Kosta's scowls were all the answers they needed. Zara didn't know what an alpha voice was, but she could guess.

Ladies, we need to have some more coffee. Would you please take the coffee into my sitting room so we can discuss what kind of coffee we want to have?

Heli stood up immediately. "Coffee? Holy crap. Okay. Let's do this."

Kosta frowned at her. "What are you all so excited about over having coffee and saying the word over and over. I mean, I get caffeine—"

"I'll fill you in later, sweetheart. Now, shoo. The girls have to have some coffee talk."

Max's eyes glowed as he glared at the lot of them. "Niko is in danger, this doesn't seem like the right time for—"

Gal nipped Max behind the knee and growled at him.

"Fine. Sorry, *kiska*. Come find me when you're done with your caffeine fix." Max waved to Kosta and they went back out the way they came.

Once they were out of sight, Selena and Gal shifted into their human forms. Selena opened a small closet near the refrigerator and pulled out two robes. She handed one to Gal and wrapped the other around herself. "You'll learn to keep stock in easy on - easy off clothing. Now come with me."

"What's happening?" Zara stood with the rest of them, not understanding why they couldn't have coffee here in the kitchen.

Heli grabbed her by the elbow and whispered, "Coffee is wolftress code for going on the attack. I'll fill you in on more of the food codes later. It's kind of my favorite part of being a wolf's mate. Especially since I didn't get the ability to shift."

They all went into Selena's bedroom and then a tastefully decorated little room off to the side with comfy chairs and a lot of books. Selena waited until they were all seated and then rubbed her hands together. "Ladies, I'm swearing you here and now to complete secrecy about what you're about to hear. No wolftress has ever broken this code in thousands of years, and I expect you all to keep that tradition going. Do you agree?"

They all nodded or said yes.

"Good. Zara, all alpha wolves have the power to compel members of their packs to their will by using something we call their alpha voice. It can't be used to make anyone hurt themselves, but it's pretty much free rein beyond that."

"I don't like the sound of that. Niko has this alpha voice?"

"He does, and his is more powerful than any other wolf."

"Why?"

"That explanation will have to come later, but know it's because of his service in Russia."

"I don't like it, but okay. What does any of this have to do with me? Do I have something like that too?"

"No. For generations, matriarchs of packs have had a complementary power, and we've kept it a secret so as to amplify its usefulness. The voice does not work on an alpha's mate. You're the only person in the world who he cannot use his power on. You are the one who can save him."

Zara looked around the room at each of the women. Violet stared at her and said, "Choose wisely."

NEW MOON PRISON

*N*iko stared at the big house in the middle of the Crescent Bay compound on Cape Cod. Getting onto their property had been too easy. He shouldn't have even made it within a mile of their pack's borders without being met by a whole contingency of enforcers.

If Ramsey was plotting to take over the world, maybe his minions had more important duties than watching for a non-threat like him. Either that, or they knew exactly where he was and were waiting to make their move. They'd made a mistake in letting him scout out the area and watch their movements.

He may not have the ability to shift into a wolf anymore and use his supernatural senses, but he had trained as an elite warrior with the Volkovs for almost eight years. The Tzar's personal guard made Navy SEALs look like Boy Scouts.

Even that hadn't been enough to save Mik.

It likely wouldn't save Niko either.

He sat in a tree watching the comings and goings, looking for any weaknesses. He'd probably missed half a dozen

already. His head just wasn't in the game and that was dangerous. He simply couldn't stop his mind from wandering to
thoughts of Zara.

What was she doing now? Had she woken to find him
gone and been mad, or maybe glad? Had Max and Kosta
broken the news to her that he'd left? Again.

His skin literally itched with the need to touch her, hold
her. He was such a dumbass for not staying with her. They
could be curled up together in his bed, her soft curves against
his hard lines. He could lose himself in her body and...

Fuck, his imagination was getting the best of him. He
could swear he smelled her unique scent of caramel and old
books. If he wasn't careful, he was going to walk into the
Crescent compound with a giant tent in his pants.

"Niko?"

Great, he was missing Zara so much, now he was hearing
her voice in his head.

"Seriously? You're in a tree? I thought you were a wolf-
shifter not a squirrel-shifter."

Shit. That wasn't in his mind. Zara was here, in enemy
territory. He searched the ground below him and didn't see
her at first. Her eyes were what gave her away. She was
dressed all in black, even covering her pretty long hair with a
dark beanie. She was so adorable in her little spy get up, he
almost hated to ruin her night.

That's exactly what he was going to do though, because she
was not staying. Dammit, His brothers were supposed take
care of her. Her showing up a stone's throw from the man
who'd kidnapped her was not what he'd meant. Fucktards.

He dropped down out of the tree and landed directly in

front of her. "What do you think you're doing here, Zara? Go home, right now."

Not nice, not friendly, not welcoming. If he was going to keep her out of trouble, he needed to embody a gruff coolness around her from here on out. He could never ever let her get even a hint of the feelings he had for her.

"Don't try to use your alpha voice on me, buster. I'm a lawyer, I can twist anything you say to benefit my side. Trust me."

After all these years, Max and Kosta were still stinking tattle tales. He should have known. "I see. You must have used your powers of persuasion on them if they let you out of their sight. I specifically told them to keep an eye on you."

"I believe your words were to take care of me. They're doing exactly that by helping me locate you. You're not taking down Ramsey Crescent without me."

He really, really shouldn't find this whole scenario sexy as hell. The fact that she'd manipulated his family and figured out how to not only search him out, but also wanted to make sure a bad man came to justice had him looking at her more as a badass and not a damsel in distress.

She wasn't entirely the fragile, innocent crusader whose tears had broken his damn heart all those years ago. She was so much more. All the more reason to ensure she was as far away from the one-blood assholes who would use her for their own gain.

There was a new clarity to her eyes and a fire in them. Calm distance wouldn't convince her to leave him to the responsibility of destroying Ramsey Crescent alone. Niko wrapped a hand around the back of Zara's neck and pushed his fingers into lush locks. He gave her hair the slightest tug, tipping her head up and exposing her throat to him.

Her eyes went dark and her pulse visibly jumped. No way she was scared of him, which meant he'd either surprised her or she was turned on by this tiny act of dominance. Christ, he needed her in so many ways.

"You're not going anywhere near Crescent." His voice came out much darker than intended.

A gorgeous fire lit in her eyes at being told what she couldn't do. "Only close enough to kill him."

Good God, he'd love the chance to stoke the flames in her. "You try, and you'll be dead before you can blink. He's a powerful alpha, and while I realize you're not a delicate fucking flower anymore, he will eat your heart for a midnight snack. I can't allow that to happen."

Zara didn't even flinch. "You think I don't see you, Nikolai Piotryvich Troika, but I do. I know you believe you're doing the right thing to make up for some kind of sins. But if sacrificing yourself because of me, it's not going to change anything."

Her vehemence struck him in the gut like a sucker-punch. She'd fucking nailed him. He'd tried hard to bury the truth under the guise of protecting his family, his friends, his pack. Only Zara could dig through all his bullshit to the core of his real intentions.

If he could eliminate everything in her life that hurt, if he could protect her from the darkness in the world and himself, maybe she could love him again. Maybe he could be worthy of her love. The love he'd lost… thrown away.

Zara saw right through him and declared it was never

going to happen. His actions wouldn't change the past, his transgressions, or her feelings for him.

He released her hair and stepped away, shoving the ache for her so far down only his wolf would be able to find it. "Then why are you here?"

"Your mother, Heli and Gal gave me quite the education a couple of hours ago. You're my fated mate, dummy. I'm not letting you go off and kill yourself." She poked him in the chest. Hard.

The tiniest ray of sunshine broke through the storm that Niko had been living in for so long. Was there actually a chance they could find happiness together? He'd run away with her right this second if that were true. "*Solnyshka.*"

The hair on the back of Niko's neck stood up on end. They were no longer alone.

"Isn't that special?" Ramsey Crescent's voice floated through the trees.

Fuck. Niko shoved Zara aside. "Zara, run. Now. I'll hold them off as long as I can."

Instead of running she slid her hand into his. "I'm not leaving you. We're in this together. Don't try to push me away again."

Ramsey stepped out of the shadows along with a whole crew of enforcers. He snapped his fingers and four of them grabbed Niko and Zara, one on each side of them. "No shifting, Troika, or my boys will do the same and your sass-mouthed girlfriend will likely get injured. Badly."

At least he still had the advantage of no one but his brothers knowing he couldn't shift. "Fine, but your enforcers leave even the lightest bruise on her, and I can't guarantee they'll continue to breathe."

"I'd rather not have to hurt her. She's going to come in very handy when I'm Tzar."

Zara huffed out an annoyed sigh. "I suppose it will be fun for me to predict the exact moment when our friend here learns to pull his head out of his ass."

Ramsey approached them and lifted Zara's face with a finger under her chin. "Coming into your own, are you, witch? Good. I wasn't looking forward to fucking a limp rag during our mating under the full moon."

"I'm not the one who needs to worry about being limp."

Ramsey raised his hand, open and ready to slap Zara. Niko tore himself out of the hold of the enforcers and snagged Crescent's arm in mid-air. His claws wrapped around the asshole's wrist, poking into, but not piercing his skin. "Don't touch her again or all bets are off. That includes your challenge. I would be well within my rights to destroy you for even threatening the woman I have marked as my own."

Ramsey tore his arm away and pointed to Zara's shoulder. "She bears no mark."

"She does. Mine."

"I never should have left you alone with her for a god-damned minute. I had every intention of making this challenge fair. I don't want anyone questioning my rule, but you've changed the rules by marking her since we agreed to the conditions. I guess I should have expected no better from the likes of you."

"If you were fucking paying attention, you would have known Zara has been mine well before I left to do my duty to the Tzar. My claim on her precedes your challenge by eight years."

Ramsey's eyes went wide and then narrowed into an ugly

scowl. "Fine. It will be all the sweeter when I kill you and claim her then. Bring them to the compound."

Ramsey turned his back on them, threw off the shirt he was wearing and shifted, letting his wolf tear through the remainder of his clothes. He howled and was joined by dozens more wolves in the woods all around them.

The enforcers surrounding Niko and Zara gave them both a shove to follow Ramsey in the direction of the Crescent compound. They walked toward the elaborate pack house in silence.

Niko stared down at his hand. He flexed his fingers and then formed a fist. It looked normal now, but he hadn't imagined his wolf's claws a moment ago. He searched inside of himself for the mental connection to his beast. There was nothing there.

Zara grabbed his fist and peeled each digit open until she fit her hand in his. She didn't say a word, but her simple touch helped more than anything else could have.

If he hadn't screwed around wondering if she loved him or not and taken her out of Crescent territory, they'd be doing a whole lot more than touching. Now he was facing death, and she wasn't going to fare much better if Ramsey's threats were to be believed.

"No one can say that I wasn't a good host for the challenge. You'll stay in one of our guest rooms until the new moon."

Guest room, his ass. "Sounds like I'm your prisoner."

"You are not, but I won't have you interfering in my pack's business." The impatience with Nico's reluctance growled out. His control was slipping. As quickly as it reared itself, the wolf in Ramsey quieted and the cool facade of the leader was back.

"You can take your meals with us if you choose, and of course you could always forfeit."

Forfeiting a challenge meant a swift death rather than a full-out battle. "Good try, Crescent. Trying to get out of fighting me for your place?"

Ramsey didn't answer him and instead addressed Zara. "You will stay with my recalcitrant daughter, witch. I'll not let you out of sight of anyone in my pack again. Unless you'd prefer my room and get a taste of a real wolf's bite."

Taryn Crescent stood on the landing above them. "Don't be disgusting, father. Come with me, Zara."

Zara glanced at Niko, and he nodded to her. He'd known Taryn for years, and she often disagreed with what her father wanted for the pack, or at least she had before he'd gone off to serve the Tzar. Granted she'd been more of an unruly teenager back then and less the grown wolftress she was now. She sure sounded like she still had that rebellious streak in her and that gave Niko the tiniest shimmer of hope that Zara might be okay if he didn't live through the night.

Once Taryn and Zara were out of sight, Ramsey muttered under his breath. "May you never be blessed with daughters."

Niko covered his snort-laughter with a cough. Good to see someone was around to keep this tyrant in line. Wolf society was a couple hundred years behind the times when it came to women's rights, so it would be hard for a headstrong woman like Taryn to make any real change in her pack. At least she was trying.

He'd like to count her as an ally, but he wasn't sure about her. Later he'd try to sneak out of his room and check in on Zara. Maybe then he could see where the Crescent heir's allegiances lay.

"It's too bad one of you boys didn't mate Taryn as your father and I planned. Then we'd be on the same side of this pack war instead of against each other."

"Hmm." That's all Niko had to say about that. He questioned every interaction his parents had with the wolf world now. They'd both known far more and had machinations that were only recently revealed. The alliance with the Crescent Bay pack could have been one more of his mother's ploys.

"I could still make that happen, you know." Ramsey threw that offer out like a tasty treat. "We can call this whole challenge off if you agree to mate my daughter."

Once again, Ramsey was giving Niko an out. This one was considerably more reasonable. He didn't want to fight Niko.

A tingling sensation at the end of his fingers that signaled his wolf's claws wanting to come out to play danced along the tips from thumb to pinky.

Ramsey Crescent wasn't simply reluctant, the bitter scent of fear floated in the air between them. That realization made Niko's need to tear the man's throat out right now skitter through his psyche. That feeling would be his advantage, and he'd utilize it as long as he could.

Intimidation was a tool like any other in his arsenal. He'd use any and every weapon he could access. "I have already marked my choice in mates."

"Marks don't mean as much as you might think in today's society. My wolves have marked a dozen or so humans just so we could see what powers they developed. It's been an interesting experiment."

Niko's instincts roared and threw Ramsey against the wall. "The only reason you're still breathing, you piece of shit, is my misplaced sense of duty to the ideals of Tzar Mikhail Volkov.

But I'd suggest you think carefully before you spout your vitriol around me again."

Crescent thrashed against Niko's arm pinning him in place. "Take him away."

Niko released the asshole and held up his hands to ward off the enforcers coming for him. "Don't bother. Point me in the right direction. I'll find my own way."

"End of the hall," the closest one said and indicated toward a hallway off the main room.

Niko turned his back on the whole group, which was a hell of a risk after what he'd pulled. Satisfaction rippled through him when none dared follow. He found the entrance to what looked like a fairly nondescript guest room right where the enforcer had said it would be. He shut the door behind him and leaned against it, taking a few breaths to calm himself.

There had to be a way to stop Ramsey Crescent from becoming Tzar without risking his own life in the process. Niko crossed the space and caught a glimpse of himself in the mirror over a small desk on one wall. His eyes were glowing.

Anticipation lit in his chest like first rays of the full moon.

He wouldn't hope for help from his wolf just yet. This was probably a fluke with his emotions running so high. That's exactly what he felt like, high on the best kind of uppers. His heart raced, his skin prickled with each flex of his muscles.

These were all signs of his long missing wolf. His mind was too empty for that to be true. No. Niko couldn't count on any favors from the Goddess. His best course of action was to find Zara.

When he was with her, everything made more sense.

He listened close until dawn came and the house went quiet as the wolves of this pack settled down to sleep the day away. If he'd been thinking clear when he'd come in here, he would have left the door open a crack. He slowly twisted the doorknob intending to do a little recon of the hallway.

Instead of an empty hall, he found Zara standing in front of him staring up with longing in her gaze. She smiled and it took his heart and blew it up like a helium balloon.

She slipped into his room, grabbed him around the neck and pulled him in for the hottest kiss of his entire life.

THE COUPLE THAT SLAYS TOGETHER

Zara was beyond stressed out being back in the Crescent Pack house, aka Casa del Crazy. Last time she'd been here her mind concluded that most of the things that went bump in the night were imaginary.

Since she'd learned that werewolves were real and were the ones who'd kidnapped her, she was more than a little freaked out. Ignorance was not bliss. It helped that Taryn Crescent was on their side.

She'd seen the extreme plans her father made in his ambition to rise in power before this pack war started escalating. She didn't want him deciding her future, much less those all wolfkind. The only problem was, Taryn didn't understand that her father would have to die.

Regardless of whether Ramsey Crescent was a human or a flying purple people eater, Zara was still determined to take him out and rescue the other women he'd captured. Since he was a werewolf, she was going to need Niko's help to accomplish that.

It left her warm and fuzzy to know they were on the same side and had a similar goal. The couple that slays together, stays together and all that.

Zara wasn't raised to believe violence was the way to change the world. Her parents were activists in anti-war movements, they recycled, planted trees, and baked cookies for protesters. None of which made a god-damned bit of difference. Fighting for human rights was important, no doubt. It was why she'd become a lawyer in the first place.

Saving actual human lives turned out to be infinitely more important when her life, and the others around her, was threatened. By freaking werewolves.

Okay. She needed to calm down about the whole werewolf thing. They couldn't be all bad if Niko and the rest of the Troikas were shifters, too. Her best friend was a shifter now. Her sister was engaged to one. She would not condemn based on their species alone, that would be fucking racist. No, Zara would be judge, jury, and executioner only for those that used their agenda to spread hate and fear to gain power.

This was why she hated politics. She wouldn't play that game. Zara was going to make things happen.

Like right now. She snuck through the servants' corridor and down to the main level of the house. Niko's bedroom should be near the front of the house according to the napkin map Taryn had drawn for her.

She peeked into the hallway and wished that the night hadn't slipped away. It didn't really matter, light or dark, the wolves would be able to see her with their fancy supernatural wolf eyesight. She needed to get her some of that. Maybe if she got Niko to bite her again.

Oooh.

No.

Maybe?

No.

She and Niko may be fated mates or whatever, but that didn't mean she should to let him all the way back into her heart. He needed to stay far, far away from the part he'd broken last time. She was willing to admit a lot of those tears and shreds of her heart were healed now that she knew so much more of the truth of what had happened.

Zara did have feelings for Niko. How could she not? But they had to take their new relationship slow and build trust again. No faster than a snail with nowhere to go, taking a nap, in molasses in January. Which meant there was no way she was sleeping with him anytime soon.

Now that she'd settled that in her mind she slipped into the quiet hallway and steeled herself to go sneak into his room. Where there was a big soft bed, and he was probably asleep. Naked.

Stop it.

She reached for handle and without even touching it, the door magically opened with Niko standing in the entry way staring down at her with an amber glow in his eyes. God, he was so damn lickable. Zara couldn't help but smile up at him.

Her skin tingled and her stomach flip-flopped. Dammit. Screw her resolve to be responsible with her heart. It belonged to Niko and always had. She'd been fooling herself to think any other way, and she wasn't a fool anymore. Zara wrapped her arms around Niko's neck and pulled him down to show him exactly what she wanted from him.

The moment their lips touched, the butterflies in her stomach rioted and sent up signal flares to her girly bits that it was go time. She wanted Niko more than anything else in her life, and that included chocolate.

Niko got the message real fast and groaned deep and low, pulling her body tight to his and sweeping his tongue into her mouth. He took over the kiss, sucking at her tongue and her lips, nipping at the corners, and making her forget how to breathe.

"Zara. Goddess, how I've dreamed of this." He lifted her up so her legs wrapped around his waist and kicked the door shut with his foot.

With Niko, she never had to worry that she was too big or heavy for him, even with her plus-size butt. She could revel in the feeling of being held by him or pressed up against the wall like he was doing now.

He grabbed her arms from around his neck and shoved them over her head. "I need you so much right now, but I don't want to hurt you or scare you. Is this what you want?"

"I want you." They both knew full well it was a risk to be together like this, under their enemies' roof, but it was now or never, and she'd already lost him once. She wasn't going to miss any opportunity to be with him. "We don't know what the day will bring, and I don't want any more regrets."

Niko nodded. and brushed his lips against hers again in agreement. "We may not have long, but I'll take whatever we get."

His eyes roamed over her body, and he gripped her hands tighter in his.

"I'm not the same boy who fumbled around in your

panties in high school." He ground his hips against her and in this position, she could feel every inch of his hard cock through their clothing. "I know how to make you scream my name when you're coming and that's only the foreplay. My tastes have grown quite a bit darker, and I'm ravenous for you, solnyshka."

"I don't care if you fumble or rock my world or insist I call you 'sir', all I want is you. You're all I ever wanted."

"Would you like it if I demanded you submit to me, Zara? If I took charge of all your pleasure and made it mine?" The glow in Niko's eyes intensified and the magic behind them swirled, until she wasn't just looking into his soul. Another presence, a part of Niko she'd never known before, peered back at her.

For the first time ever, she was seeing his wolf. His body hadn't changed, his face was still human, but inside something so much more than a mere man waited for her answer.

Zara's entire body flushed as she warmed from the inside out. She was seeing his true self, and it was so perfect and beautiful. "I want you to make all of me yours, Niko. My pleasure, my need, my heart, my soul. Take it all from me and take it for your own."

"You are already mine. You always have been." Niko growled and fangs extended from his mouth. "Mine."

He bent his head to her throat and scraped his teeth across her pulse point, not breaking the skin, but sending a shiver through her whole body. She didn't know why, but she knew down to her soul that she needed him to bite her, that it would somehow make her his in more than words.

Zara squirmed against him, wanting her hands free from

his tight grasp so she could pull his head back to her neck and feel his teeth on her again. "Please, Niko. I need—"

"I know everything you need, and I'll give it to you when we're both good and ready. Trust me with your body and your heart. You don't have to worry about anything anymore. I'm going to cherish and protect you now and for as long as we have together."

Zara planned for that to be forever, and she wouldn't take anything less. She licked her lips and, since getting her hands back from him didn't seem like an option, wiggled her hips. "Let's not waste a second."

He grinned. "Is that your way of telling me to hurry up and rip your clothes off?"

"Get my clothes off, get me off, you know, all of the above." She enjoyed flirting with him. It had been such a long time since she'd even had fluttery feelings like this. It was a hell of a lot better than worrying she was going crazy.

Niko wrapped his hands under her butt and carried her across to the bed. He pushed her into the mattress with his body and oh so slowly pulled her shirt up and over her head. His eyes roamed over her chest, following the line of her bra.

She wished for a moment her bra and panties something cute and frilly. But it wasn't like she'd known they were going to get naked when putting on basic black undergarments. He took his own sweet time examining every inch of her and hooked his fingers under the straps, pulling them down her arms. She almost wanted him to rip it off of her, but then she would be left without a bra, and she was not letting her girls run free near all these stupid wolves.

Niko's tongue darted out when he licked his lips, and she couldn't wait for him to get that tongue on her body. Zara unhooked her knees from around his hips, but he grabbed her thighs and dug his fingers in, holding her in place. "Don't move your legs even an inch."

He ground his cock against her again. She was going to scream from frustration, which was not what she was promised. She really needed him to get his show on her road. "This would be more fun if we weren't wearing pants."

He got a look on his face that was so cocky, it couldn't help but be toe-curling hot with the promises it made. "Too late to decide you wanted to be in control."

To punctuate his declaration, he reached around and popped the clasp of her bra open without even a glance at what he was doing.

For once in her life, she couldn't wait to not be in charge. It was freaking exhausting to always be on and responsible, to make everything happen the right way. She fully understood that wanting to be a strong, independent woman didn't have to be at odds with letting her man take charge of her pleasure in the bedroom.

In fact, it was the greatest form of self-care to be able to let go for a little while and be allowed to simply feel and enjoy. That wasn't anti-feminist. That was smart.

The weight of the world lifted from her chest along with her bra, and, for the first time in years, she could breathe again. "Thank goodness."

Niko brushed the back of his fingers so softly over her breasts and nipples that they hardened and poked up simply to be closer to him. He bent his head and licked one and then the other, giving it the tiniest tug between his teeth. His hands wandered down her bare sides and to her hips and finally cupped her ass, dragging her body even closer to his. "I'd love to tie you up, lay you across my lap, and spank the hell out of this plush ass for scaring the shit out of me by showing up here."

Her senses fired up everywhere his skin touched hers. "Nobody is stopping you."

"I am." He stared into her eyes, holding her gaze for several breaths. "This might be the only chance we have to be together. I want to do everything with you, but I won't compromise your safety just to get off."

At least she wasn't the one who said they may not live through this. She couldn't love him any more for understanding that. "Then let's make this time count."

His grip on her butt and hips got all possessive. "Grab onto the headboard, and don't let go unless I tell you to. Understand?"

Why, oh why was Niko telling her what to do so fricking hot? He'd barely even touched her yet and when he finally did make it to the clothes removal portion of the night, he was going to find her panties pretty well soaked. Zara reached behind her head and gripped the wood. That position arched her back and thrust her breasts forward, and she became sex on a stick for him.

"If I ever get to bring you home to my own bed, I'll take my time finding out exactly how hard I can get those plump little nipples of yours. They'll look so good with clamps to decorate and stimulate them. I'll be spending a very long time with my cock between those tits." He sucked in a breath between his teeth looking her over. "Before I do anything else, I've been waiting a far too long to lay my mouth on the mark I gave you once again."

Niko wrapped his fingers into the waistband of her yoga

pants and pulled them and her black panties down her hips. She lifted her bum to help him out, and in a second she was naked and laid out for him.

Eight years was a long time, and she wasn't a bright-eyed teenage girl anymore. She didn't have that body either. A lot of hours in the office with no exercise and crap food coupled with a stupid amount of stress and the fact that she'd already been chubby in high school meant her ass had spread, and she had more than a couple love handles, not to mention jiggly thighs.

"Christ, you're fucking gorgeous." His gaze perused its way up and down her body, taking in all the lumps, bumps, flaws, pooches, and sags. Yet not once did he look disappointed or resigned. In fact, with every second that passed, his eyes darkened and sparkled, the lust practically pouring out of them for her. All for her.

"You make me feel beautiful." He always had, and she'd forgotten that.

She hoped he wouldn't keep her waiting too long before she got her chance to touch him and explore his body too. But the way the wolf in him kept flashing a hungry, lustful need at her, she wasn't sure she would be allowed to do much more than anticipate his orders.

"Spread your legs for me and let me see it, Zara."

A shiver of pure desire rolled through her from her toes up, and she squeezed the headboard tight. She'd dreamed of this moment with Niko more often than she wanted to admit.

"Show me the mark I gave you and your sweet, wet cunt."

Zara let her knees fall open and tilted her right thigh, so the amber moon with the silhouette of a white wolf howling in the center faced up. She'd never understood where it came from. Deep down, she would never admit that it had always made her feel connected to Niko.

A rumble sounded from his chest and his fangs extended down over his lips. She hadn't seen him appear so animalistic before, and she absolutely loved every bit of this dominating alpha side of him.

MARKED BY THE ALPHA

*C*lear as the most brilliant diamond, the image of a white wolf inside a full moon shined up from between Zara's legs. His mark. He'd given her that symbol of their joined fate eight years ago.

He hadn't known it at the time, and he didn't mean to bite and mark her. Biting a human was not only strictly forbidden, it was the most taboo act a wolf could do. Niko hadn't even realized he'd done it until after they'd both come in the most erotic moment he'd ever experienced.

Laying there with his cock in her mouth, seeing the wound he'd given her, he should have been horrified with himself. He'd drawn blood, and he could already see she would bruise. Instead of the revulsion that should have coursed through him, his dick went instantly hard for the second time that night.

He licked the bite mark to soothe any sting, but he couldn't resist licking her sweet pussy too. She'd moaned around his cock, and they'd gone at it again.

Laying together in the back of his car, basking in their

afterglow, he'd asked her to marry him. Even though he knew it wasn't what his parents wanted for him or the pack. He hadn't been thinking about the consequences of being the heir to the alpha, only how much he loved her.

That was the last moment the two of them had been happy together. The shitshow started right after that.

Everything had changed after that. Him most of all.

Seeing his mark on her skin now brought something of his old self back. That part of him that thought he and Zara could change the world, make it a better place for both humans and wolves, woke up from its long coma. Maybe if they were together once again, working side by side, they could not only save themselves, but this strange future they'd found themselves in.

His emotions were too overwhelming for him to be able to say the words to her yet. He needed to burn off some of this fierce energy burning through him right now. The best way he knew how to do that was orgasms. Lots and lots of screaming orgasms.

Niko lowered his head and licked the mark on her, just as he'd done all those years ago. He could feel the minutely raised flesh of her scarred skin where his teeth had punctured. She whimpered with the same needy tone he remembered from the many nights he'd replayed the memory of their last night together.

But Zara was no mere teenager anymore. Her curves were even more lush than before, her breasts fuller, and her hips and ass were perfect for holding tight in his fists when he thrust into her. Later. She would come first. Always.

He'd learned a hell of a lot about how to drive a woman not only crazy with his attention to her body, but he could send even the toughest submissive into subspace when he wanted to. Mik had introduced him to the gratification and satisfaction of domination and submission in one of the Volkovs' many clubs. Niko had learned exactly how to dominate anyone with pleasure, pain, denial, and ecstasy.

His wolf had always reveled in this kind of sex play, bringing a whole new aspect to being an alpha. One that he sorely wished to share with Zara.

"Please don't tease me like this, Niko. Don't make me wait anymore. I need to feel your mouth on me."

Sweet Zara was trying so hard to let him take charge, and he'd gotten lost in his own reminisces, like an asshole. "You'll wait as long as I want. The anticipation makes it all the more delicious when I do this." He swiped his tongue up one of her pussy lips and down the other, very purposefully avoiding her clit.

She groaned and the headboard creaked as she adjusted her grip on it. He was going to have so much fun driving her crazy with lust and need. They had a lot of lost time to make up for.

Niko spread her legs wider and nibbled his way up her thigh, spending plenty of time licking, nipping, and dragging his teeth across her mark. Her pussy glistened with her juices, called to him like the most delicious treat. He licked her vulva again and then pressed the flat of his tongue against the very center of her core, flexing and thrusting against her.

"Oh God, Niko. Holy..." her words became incoherent, and he chuckled, loving that he could make her lose her ability to speak with only a touch. His tongue was only the beginning of the pleasure he had in store for them both. He swirled around and around, up and down, and sucked on her tight nub until her legs were shaking and he could feel the flutters of her pussy signaling her impending orgasm. Her breathing was coming in ragged gasps, and he could literally hear her heart racing.

He slipped two fingers into her tight cunt and replaced his tongue with his thumb, pressing down on the quivering bundle of nerves. "This is mine now, *malyshka*. Your orgasm is mine, your beautiful cunt is mine, and you'll give me your pleasure when I tell you to. Not a moment before."

Her eyes were shut and the skin on her thighs, belly, breasts, and cheeks flushed. "Niko... please."

"Mine, Zara. Your body is mine." Every cell of his being screamed at him to claim her now, mark her where everyone could see and make her cry out his name as he fucked her. Niko had a lot of experience in denying himself in favor of seeing his partner submit to his will.

She jerkily nodded and pressed her hips against his hand.

"That's my girl." She was so much more than a girl, or even a woman, to him. She was his mate. He hadn't been sure he would get to have a true mate once he'd gone into service for Mik and the Volkovs. He'd given up everything, lost it all. Having Zara here, belonging to him once again body and soul, was a blessing he would have to spend the rest of his pitiful life thanking the Goddess for.

One more reason to make sure they both lived through the challenge.

Something he would worry about tomorrow. Today was theirs no matter what happened.

Zara opened her eyes and stared up at him with so much love in gaze, every plan he had to dominate her mind and body flew out the window and crashed on the rocks below. If he didn't get inside of her right now and feel her cunt squeezing his cock as he pumped his seed into her, he was going to explode, or implode, or maybe just blow his load. None of which he wanted to do.

As much as his own desire raged through his loins, he would not give in to his own hedonism unless Zara was with him all the way. He could fuck her right here and now, but until he let her see all of him, he wasn't being honest with her. They were fated mates, he knew that to the very core of his soul, but he wouldn't force her to be with him.

It was her choice if she wanted to hitch her star to someone so broken and damned as he.

"*Solnyshka*, I want nothing more than to mark and claim you, to fill your body until neither of us knows what it's like to be apart, but you need to know—"

"Niko." She lifted her chin. "I do. I know everything there is to know about you. Even if fate or destiny or whatever you want to believe in wasn't involved, we would still be together. I would always choose you."

He wanted so much for that to be true. "I've… done things, I'm not the man you think I am."

"Look into my eyes and listen to me. Nikolai, I know. Neither of us understood then, but you gave me a gift. The gift to be with you even when we were apart. I've watched almost everything you've been through for the past eight years as if we were together the whole time."

Her visions. Holy shit. "Everything?"

Her expression softened. "Not every second of every day, but all the important bits. I thought I was dreaming, or day-dreaming, or hallucinating, and I don't completely understand it all, but I saw most of the significant events in your life before they even happened."

"Even..." He swallowed and looked away. His next words came out as cracked as his soul. "Even Mik's death?"

Zara let go of the headboard and sat up. She got onto her knees and grabbed his face between her palms. Her gaze flicked back and forth, studying him. His chest tightened until his lungs stopped working.

"I think I've seen more about what happened to you and Mikhail than you have."

It was true that he'd blocked a lot of that night from his memory. He couldn't bring himself to remember murdering his best friend. Mik's blood was on his hands. He avoided looking her in the eyes. His shame was far too great.

"Do you want me to tell you what I saw?" She whispered.

Self-revulsion roiled in his gut. "No, I can't."

"Yet... You can't face it yet, and I certainly won't force you." She squeezed his shoulder. "But when you're ready, we'll deal with it together."

Zara had more faith in him than he did. He hated to continue to ruin it. "There's more."

"There isn't anything you can say that will make me stop loving you." She laid her cheek against his.

Sure there was. Wait... Love? Did she just say... out loud... that she loved him? He could face his demons if that were true.

What if he didn't tell her? They could run away together, escaping the Crescent compound wouldn't be easy, but they could do it. They could leave all of wolfkind behind and never look back.

He would think about that tomorrow.

This time when he thought that, it didn't give him the same relief as usual. The idea of giving up their future because he was scared of facing life as less than a true alpha wolf burned in his chest.

Man up, since he couldn't wolf up. "I can't protect you. If you throw in with me, you're choosing a mate that will never fulfill his duties to keep you safe and give you the life you deserve."

She took a breath and opened her mouth to interrupt him, but he pressed a finger to her lips. "I can't shift, Zara. I've lost my wolf, and I don't know if I'll ever get it back. If I try to fight Crescent in the challenge, he will tear me apart, and then he'll claim you. I won't condemn you to a torturous life with a bastard like him."

Zara tisked. "You've gotten really good at lying to yourself."

He expected anger, but... umm, what? "I'm not. I wouldn't lie to you."

"Not to me, to yourself. You haven't lost anything. I've been staring into the eyes of your wolf since we kissed. Look." She turned him toward the mirror he'd caught a glimpse of himself in before.

He'd truly thought the supernatural glow was a momentary fluke, nothing more than a response to their dire situation. Looking into the mirror, with Zara staring back at him over his shoulder, he couldn't deny that she was correct. Wavering across his own features, in his eyes, but more than that, in his entire being, he could see his white wolf.

Niko closed his eyes and reached inside for the connection to his beast, to the vital part of him that made him who he was and was meant to be. He still received no answer to his plea for the wolf to appear, to make itself known to him again, but the place that used to feel hollow, had changed.

Instead of a dark black hole sucking away his energy, his happiness, and his life, a new power surged there. He didn't understand what it was or how to access it, only that where he was once shattered pieces, he was whole.

"Did you do this? Did you somehow heal me?" Shock and awe coursed through him like electricity.

Zara giggled and gave him a quick little kiss. "I've got some X-men level superpowers, but I don't think healing is one of them."

"Maybe not, but whatever this is, it's because of you, because you love me." He was incredibly awed just to be near her, for her to allow him into her life, much less have these kinds of feelings for him. His heart was growing three times, more and more, like the Grinch.

"Love conquers all?"

"Love is going to conquer you. Come here." He pulled her into his arms and kissed her soundly. He wasn't ever gonna let her go.

The kiss rapidly turned hot, and he could literally taste the spice of her need in his mouth. He'd stopped their love making in the middle when she was on the verge of coming which certainly wasn't very nice of him. He would remedy that immediately, if not sooner.

"On your hands and knees, Zara. It's time I showed your body exactly why it belongs to me."

Her eyes sparkled, and her pupils went wide as her mind responded to his command. She licked her lips and let out the tiniest, "Ohh."

She sat back, with her palms on her thighs in the perfect

submissive pose and the new power in him surged at the sight. She was only in the position for an instant while in the process of moving onto all fours like he'd told her to, but it was long enough for him to recognize it as something they both wanted and would spend a lot of time exploring some-time very soon.

This wasn't about domination and submission, even though it was roles they were clearly made to be in, compli-menting each other. Right now was about marking her for all the world to see, claiming her, with the intention to make her his mate. The sooner the better.

"The more you think about it, the longer you'll wait to come." They were both coming in the next three and a half minutes, but she didn't need to know that.

Zara rolled to her hands and knees on the bed and shook her bare ass at him. He couldn't resist. He slapped her right butt cheek in one fast and hard spank. Even the loud crack of his hand to her soft flesh didn't cover her moan. He was going to have so much fun playing that game between pleasure and pain with her.

"Head down, ass up." His cock was straining against his jeans to get to her body. It had been so long since he'd allowed himself to be inside any woman's cunt, ass, or mouth. He couldn't bring himself to fuck the women in the Volkovs' clubs. It never felt right. Play with them, yes. Make them come, absolutely. Put his cock in them. Not so much.

His hands shook with the slightest tremor as he unbuckled and dropped his pants to the floor. He threw his shirt over his shoulders, wanting as much of his skin as possible to touch hers when he took her. Fucked her.

Niko crawled onto the bed behind her and slipped two

fingers into her wet cunt, pulling her juices out and preparing her body to take him. He coated her flesh and his fingers, then grabbed his own cock and spread her essence all along his shaft. The wetter the better. He wasn't shy about being very well-endowed, and she was tight as fuck.

He placed his cock at her entrance and teased her by not pushing in.

She wiggled her ass and tried to push back so she could take him into her body, but he grabbed her hips and held her firmly. "Please, you're killing me. I need you so badly, please."

Hearing her beg for him ignited a new surge in the power inside of him. His cock grew even bigger and harder in his hand. He slipped through her wet folds, tormenting her, sliding his tip across her clit until she was gasping for breath.

Leaning over her back, he reached around and teased her, alternating between his cock and his fingers. "Is this what you need?"

"Yes," she panted. "No. I need you inside me... Now."

There was something so hot about how bossy she got when she was on the verge of coming. "Your wish is my command."

This time when he thrust forward, it was to fill her body with his, to connect them, irrevocably. He pushed into her tight heat slowly, another inch with each breath. Her inner muscles squeezed him as she adjusted to his size. God, he was going to have to be careful with her fragile human form.

"Harder, Niko... More."

Or maybe not. Within a few thrusts he was pounding into her and Zara's hands gripped the blankets as she moaned his name. "Niko, yes, yes."

Like she had the instinct, she tipped her head to the side

exposing her neck and throat to him. The new-found power swelled and crescendoed at the sight of her total submission to him. The room swirled in an amber light, and he growled deeply just to avoid howling his gratification to the sky.

Niko sank his fangs into her soft skin and kept her shoulder tight between his teeth. Her body shook with an incredible orgasm, pulling at his own climax. He groaned and held back only by the sheer force of his will and the discipline he'd enforced on himself.

A power greater than Niko overrode his will and his cock bulged at the base, his hips drove forward on their own accord until he was seated fully inside Zara's body. They were locked together by the wolf's knot and Niko roared as he poured his seed into her, releasing years of pent-up fear, anger, lust, and love in one soul-melting claiming of his true mate.

SECRETS

*W*ow. If Zara had known not having sex for eight years would end with such a bang, she would have... done absolutely nothing different. She laid wrapped in Niko's arms, basking in the afterglow of the most amazing full-body orgasm. The two of them were breathing hard and his cock was still inside of her, filling her.

Niko groaned. "Solnyshka, are you okay?"

She was so far beyond okay. There weren't enough synonyms for okay to describe how she was doing. Good, great, fantabulous, stupendous. Nope, none of them quite did the trick. She was better than any mere words could express. "Mmm-hmm."

He laid his face on her back and kissed her shoulder. "Great, because I don't think I can move."

Zara giggled. She couldn't even remember the last time she'd spontaneously laughed. Here in the midst of a very dangerous day that was going to end in violence, Zara felt joy. Out and out joy.

That more than anything else gave her the confidence to

know that being with him was the right thing. For both of them. "I love you, Niko."

He turned her face so he could look into her eyes. "I love you so much it hurts in all the best ways."

His cock moved, growing thicker again, and Niko slid his arms underneath their bodies to stroke her clit. She'd already come so hard, she wasn't sure she had another orgasm in her. When he pushed even deeper into her pussy and made the smallest of thrusts in time to his flicks over her clit, she was moaning in under a second.

"Come for me once more, love." He whispered in her ear and scraped his teeth across her shoulder.

Zara's body went from peaceful bliss to nuclear under his touch. His cock barely moved inside of her, but he felt so incredibly big and the pressure built and built and built until her climax was right on the edge.

"Now, Zara. Come now and let me feel your cunt milk my cock." His command came out strained and his voice was so husky and filled with lust that she could hear that he was on the verge of coming too.

"Together," she managed to groan out before her body detonated, taking him with her into nirvana once again.

"Fuu-uuck, Zara." Niko's body jerked and hot seed burst from him. In unison, their bodies continued to pulse, their orgasms synced along with their heartbeats.

Niko recovered faster than she did and tried to roll them, so he wasn't on top of her anymore. "We're gonna have to lay here for another minute or, uh, I don't actually know how long."

"Hmm-kay. Not that I'm opposed, but you sound like you have a specific reason for that."

"The easiest way to put it is that the wolf isn't ready to let you go yet. I've heard other wolf-shifter men talk about it, but I didn't think that it would happen, especially since I...but you've healed me somehow." He did roll them this time, just to their sides, and his cock remained fully inside her.

"Oh, God. You feel so...." He was blessed with a dick that was, as far as she knew, larger than most, but this felt different. Not unpleasant, just, "...big."

Niko chuckled and hugged her to his chest. "I'd love to take that as a compliment, but it's the wolf's knot. Our bodies are locked together until my wolf is satisfied that you're thoroughly mine."

She wasn't sure how to soothe that part of him. Give him a pat on the head, a treat, and tell him good job? She didn't have any treats, but she did have her feelings for him. "I am yours, forever."

A tingle pricked her skin where he'd bitten her. The bite had sent her straight into orgasm both times, and this prickle was a similar feeling as that buildup of pressure before release. It almost tickled, and it definitely felt good.

"Forever," he confirmed. He kissed the spot on the back of her shoulder and pulled out of her. "Would you like to see your new mark?"

"Oh. Is that what was happening?" She jumped out of the bed and ran over to the little mirror hanging near the door. When she turned, she saw an image on her skin, similar to a tattoo, but much more brilliant, identical, but twice the size of the one between her legs.

Niko joined her and the amber light in his eyes matched the color of the moon emblazoned on her. The wolf stared out at both of them, but it wasn't just the image of his beast -

it was Niko too. Zara had seen other shifters' eyes do the glow thing, but Niko's gaze was different. His wolf and he were combined into one in that reflection in the mirror.

"You should try shifting. I'd very much like to see the animal side of you." She knew that part of him wasn't lost as he'd thought. She didn't know anything about healing a supernatural being, but she did understand wounds of the mind. Maybe his inability to be the wolf was more in his head than he assumed.

"Yeah, me too." He shrugged and stepped away. After a hard breath, Niko stood up straight, tilted his head to either side, shook his hands and bounced on each foot like a sprinter psyching himself up for a race. He closed his eyes and scrunched up his face. In another second, he opened one eye and peered over at her. "Nothing. It's not the same as before when that part of me was empty. I used to be able to call on the wolf, sense its presence and what it wanted. It's as if he's giving me the silent treatment."

"But you knew before when we were -" she waved her hand toward the bed looking for a phrase that wasn't weird, "- locked together, it was because of your wolf. How did you know that?"

His brow wrinkled while he thought. "I just did."

A howl sounded somewhere off in the distance and they both turned toward the window. The sunlight was fading, and dusk would come soon. They'd spent the day in bed instead of plotting their vengeance, umm, planning on how to defeat Ramsey Crescent.

She was glad. Being with Niko had changed that dark part of her heart that only wanted revenge. Now with a clearer mind, and some good old-fashioned teamwork, they might be able to actually do something about this take-over the world plot he seemed to have.

"We need to get you out of here, my love. I don't want you anywhere near that challenge in a few hours."

She recognized his fear and his protectiveness talking, but that's not how they were going to operate anymore. "Oh, no you don't, buster. We are together, forever... Remember?"

Niko's hands clenched at his side. "I've dreamed of a long and blissful life with you, but we might have to settle for a short and exciting one. Ramsey Crescent has to die, and I the one to end his sorry existence. I'm not sure I'll manage it without dying myself, not if my wolf won't show up to tear him apart."

"Now would be an awfully good time for one of my visions, too bad I have no idea how to—"

Boom. Zara was standing in a field in almost total darkness. No moon hung in the sky, but hundreds of eyes glowed in a circle around her. At her feet lay a golden wolf, dead, his throat cut. She looked down at her hands and they were covered in blood, holding a knife. No, not a knife, a giant claw. No that wasn't right either. Her hand was a claw.

This wasn't her own body. It was Niko's. He raised her arm up like he was going to strike at the dead beast again, but with his other hand, he gripped his own wrist in mid-air. Both arms shook with the force of fighting each other. "No. You can't make me do this."

Zara slowly backed away from the golden wolf's body. Her legs felt strange, and she realized they were not her own either. She glanced over her shoulder and realized she was mere inches from a cliff's edge. She stumbled, some force trying to draw her back toward the golden wolf, to finish the job.

"Get out of my head, you demon." It was Niko's voice that came out of her mouth.

Did he mean her?

A wolf who was not a wolf, which she didn't understand, stalked toward her, its eyes glowing with an eerie red light. Behind it a man who was also a dragon, a black one, watched them both. The wolf lowered its head and growled. Your job is already done. But I have many more plans for you, little *Rynda*.

Zara glanced over at the golden wolf's body, then go the threshold of the cliff. She had failed in her duty to protect the Tzar, she would not be used by Volkovs as their puppet. It took every smidgen of will power she had to take a step backward, then another, and another, until her foot slipped, and dirt and rock tipped over the precipice and into the black crevasse below.

She smiled then because she knew she had won. Her only regret was that she wouldn't be able to see Zara ever again. Perhaps in their next lives, if the Goddess allowed. She opened her arms wide and leaned back, trusting in nothing but the wind and snow to catch her.

The wolf-demon howled and ran to the edge of the cliff. The last thing she saw was its red eyes blink out and then there was only pain.

Somewhere in the depths of the brutal agony of his body being torn apart by rocks and the chunks of sharp ice in the river at the bottom of the gorge he'd jumped into, he found the peace of death. A white light surrounded him, and a woman spoke, her voice soft and lilting, not unlike his beautiful Zara's.

Hush yourself now, brave wolf. Rest and heal, you have many more battles ahead of you.

He did? How could he fight if he was dead? He couldn't think about that now. All he wanted was to close his eyes and bask in the warm glow of this goddess or angel or whatever she was.

Sorry, kiddo. We can't let you die. We've got plans for you. That voice was much deeper and very male. It had a ring of an alpha in it, but no alpha wolf he'd ever known sounded like that.

Come, my heart. We need to fly now and get him home before that fucking demon figures out we've foiled his plans. I can't wait until he and his sister get their come-uppance. Again.

Niko had the strangest sensation of floating through the air, as if a bird had picked him up and carried him away.

Yes, but we have a lot of work to do before that day comes. I'm afraid our little vacation is over. It's time for us to play matchmakers.

And you're sure one of these douchepotato wolves is the right mate for our little dragon daughter? I still don't know about that.

Douchepotato? Why was he a douchepotato?

He's not a potato, Kur.

He is for going and dying.

Aha. He knew he was dead. This was not quite what he'd thought the afterlife would be like though. Maybe they weren't there yet, and they were flying him to heaven?

He will be the strongest leader his people have ever seen,

and his kin will inherit the best of those qualities. Can you think of anything better for Ishtar than that? She's waited in the dark an awfully long time, and she'll need someone as powerful as she is to stand by her side in the final battle.

Niko was starting to get the feeling these were not angels, and he was not going to some promised afterlife where he could float around on clouds and pee on trees to his heart's content. Whatever happened to all wolves go to heaven?

The woman, a vision in white, hovered into view for the first time and looked directly into Zara's soul. Wake up, dear. Oh, and ask Taryn to help you. She's got some daddy issues.

Zara's eyes snapped open and she had to swallow back the nausea roiling up her throat from her wild ride. "Whoa."

"Holy shit, babe. You scared the crap out of me. Are you okay? I couldn't get you to respond, and you've been out for a long time." Niko lifted her by her shoulders and squeezed her tight.

"Oh no." She glanced at the window and it wasn't there. In fact, the whole room was gone. "Where are we?"

Taryn's face popped into view. "He brought you here when you wouldn't wake up. What did you see?"

Taryn had been here when Zara had visions before. Good, at least someone understood what was happening.

"You." That wasn't entirely correct, but she wasn't talking about what she'd actually seen with anyone but Niko.

"Me?" Taryn backed away slowly. "I don't want you to have visions about me."

"Yeah. A woman in white told me to ask you to help us defeat your father." That was not normally how her other sight worked. Usually, she saw some prophecy of the future, and they were a lot vaguer than this one. A person, or whatever that woman in what was, had never spoken directly to her before.

Taryn shook her head. "It has been made perfectly clear, I'm not good for anything but a marriage alliance. I can't defeat my father. That's what Niko is supposed to do."

There was much more to the Crescent heir than that. Zara didn't have a clear memory of everything that happened the night she'd been rescued, but she knew Taryn had led a group of women and wolves against her father. Seemed she had paid the price for that insurrection.

Zara glanced up at Niko trying a little eye-speak to tell him to say something. There had to be a reason the woman in white had chosen Taryn specifically. But as with most of her visions, there wasn't enough information to identify what to do.

Niko stared at the daughter of his enemy for an uncomfortable moment. "You can help me, Taryn Crescent."

The amber glow in his eyes illuminated and neither Zara nor Taryn could look away. "You and I both know behind every alpha is a strong matriarch. You're a wolftress, you have more power than you give yourself credit for. I've known for a long time that you should inherit this pack, not some beta from another pack who mates you for your name. Help me change the system starting here and now."

Hell, yeah. That was the piece Zara was missing. If she wanted to make sure the trafficking of women stopped, how better to do that than to put a woman in charge of the ones who were doing it? Perfect.

Taryn's expression was a bit awestruck, but she slowly nodded. "What do you want me to do?"

"Keep my secret," Niko said.

"That I can do. I've got more secrets up here," she pointed to her temple, "than anyone knows."

"Good. Then here's one more. I'm entrusting you with my life. I need your help. You must be the one to kill your father during the challenge and take over your pack." He waited until she tentatively nodded. "Because I can't shift into wolf form, and you can."

CHALLENGERS AND OTHER BAD GUYS

*N*iko snuck back to his room only moments before the Crescent enforcers came to get him for the challenge. One of them sniffed around as he undressed. There was no chance at hiding the scent of sex.

"Hope you enjoyed your last hurrah, Troika. I do have to say I'm looking forward to our alpha fucking your whore. She's got a hell of an ass on her."

Christ. If Niko could shift, this guy's head would be the first he'd rip off. If ever his wolf had an excuse to show itself, an insult to his mate should be it. But still, there was nothing. Only that sense of power that he didn't have access to. The best he could do is give a dark look that held a promise of retribution. Someday he would find a way to make this jackass eat his words.

The other enforcer stepped between the two of them. "My apologies for my pack mate. He doesn't seem to understand that you could be our alpha within the hour."

Huh. Interesting. Perhaps not all the members of Crescent were happy with their alpha. Niko would remember that when Taryn took over and let her know this particular enforcer could be of use to her in her new regime. He sure as shit hoped he'd done the right thing talking that girl into patricide.

It wasn't that uncommon for an heir to kill their own alpha in the old days. Fewer packs were quite that brutal in the twenty-first century, though. It would help Taryn establish her dominion over the people. A female alpha was beyond rare. The only other one he knew of was Galyna, Max's mate, who'd won her pack when that piece of shit alpha had tried to kill Max.

Gal and Taryn had worked closely to rescue Zara, so he was sure they'd work well together once the dust settled after this moon-forsaken challenge.

"Let's get this show on the road, shall we, boys?" Niko pulled the door open and marched down the hall. The enforcers scrambled to catch him. He'd spent time at the Crescent compound with his father many moons ago and remembered where their sacred circle was hidden.

"Keep up, enforcers. I don't have all night." His guards were visibly uncomfortable having to follow him when they should be leading him to his doom.

Ramsey Crescent wasn't a bit surprised. He already stood in the center of the circle, naked and ready to shift for the fight.

Niko wouldn't let anyone have even a hint that he wasn't fully prepared to do the same. He strolled in with all the swagger he could muster and ripped his shirt over his head. He tossed it in Zara's direction, so she'd know he saw her and Taryn waiting on the sidelines. "Sure you don't want to back out, Crescent. Now that I've had a taste for your decadence,

I'm mighty tempted to stick around awhile, take over and show your pack what a real leader does."

Ramsey didn't appreciate that one bit. "Trash like you will never lead my pack, much less wolfkind."

Perfect. If Niko could get this egotistical pile of shit riled up, he wouldn't be thinking as clearly. The Volkovs may be unscrupulous, unethical, untrustworthy despots, but their warrior training for the *Rynda* was unparalleled. That included psychological fighting techniques. Niko couldn't call on his wolf's ability, but he could still play a good head game.

With each of his words, Niko eased himself around the circle so that his back was to Zara and Taryn, doing his best to make it seem as though he was jockeying for an advantageous position. He shucked his jeans and folded his arms. He grinned right at Ramsey and waggled his brow then glanced down to draw attention to how much bigger his dick was than his opponents. "Well, I certainly can't let the werewolves of the world be turned into whiny, sniveling, crybabies like you."

Ramsey's wolf shimmered through his eyes and fur popped up on his arms and across his shoulders. "You and your brothers are the whiners who won't keep your dicks and teeth away from your human whores."

The circle gasped which showed just how deep the taboo of biting humans went in their culture. If they only knew. If Niko was very, very lucky, he'd survive long enough to prove to them all the truth of finding one's true fated mate.

A few more steps, and he was directly in front of Taryn. "Funny. I suppose you haven't mentioned to your pack that you planned to take a human mate when this was all over, did you?"

A few of the wolves around the circle grumbled, but more looked not only surprised, but interested. Oh, yeah. Ramsey Crescent had miscalculated the wants and needs of his people. He would have fit in perfectly with the Volkovs. Another reason he and his one-blood followers had to be eliminated.

The bones in Ramsey's arms popped as he transformed them into the wolf's, complete with deadly claws extended. "I never said I would mate her. But be assured, I'll fuck her so as to erase your stench from her body. Then she will serve me as I reign as Wolf Tzar."

Time for the final blow. "You can be the Tzar right after you come over here and kiss my bare fucking ass."

Ramsey shifted fully and howled at the dark sky of the new moon. *Shift, Troika, and fight me as a wolf.*

Niko crouched low as if he were about to shift, and let as much of his beast out as would show itself. His fangs dropped, his claws came out, and his vision went bright as his wolf sight took over. It was more than he could have hoped for. He growled deep, from his core. "Come at me, Crescent. Show the world you want to kill me."

Ramsey charged at Niko, teeth bared, fixed on tearing him apart. Niko didn't move a muscle, but prayed to the moon goddess in the sky that Taryn was ready behind him. Time slowed as his focus narrowed to just the wolf in front of him, the danger racing closer and closer.

He saw the second Ramsey realized Niko wasn't going to shift. The total disdain for everything Niko was and stood for was clear in his wolf's eyes and that hatred fueled his attack, putting more speed into his charge. When he was less than a foot away, Niko pounced from his crouch to a full standing position, he twisted his body, thanking the goddess his reactions were as quick as a wolf's and watched as Ramsey jumped into the air.

He wouldn't be able to pivot fast enough to catch Niko's neck in his teeth as he had planned. The look of surprise on his face intensified as he flew past Niko and toward the waiting dagger held in Taryn's outstretched hand.

It was almost too easy.

Tears streamed down Taryn's face and the knife tumbled from her hand. Zara gasped and moved faster than he would have thought possible, putting herself between the attacking alpha wolf and the daughter who would betray him. Ramsey lashed out, aiming directly for Zara's fragile neck.

Niko didn't have time to think, his hand shot out with his claws extended, his arm fully shifted into his more powerful wolf form. He struck at Ramsey's throat catching him under the chin. The momentum of the wolf's jump continued to propel him forward and Niko's claw sliced him open from chest to belly, cracking his ribs and spilling his internal organs in a spray of grisly death.

Ramsey's body fell to the ground and skidded to within an inch of Zara and Taryn.

The circle went as silent as a graveyard.

Niko watched Zara, making sure she wasn't harmed. She gave a tiny shake of her head so imperceptible no one else would have even noticed. When he was assured she was okay, he glanced at Taryn. She did not return his look, only glared down at the dead wolf at her feet.

"Claim your pack, Taryn," he whispered to her.

She still didn't face him. She shook, everything in her body rejecting the situation and her responsibility. Her only answer was to turn tail, shift into her wolf, shredding her clothes in her haste and sprint into the woods.

Fuck. That left Niko with no choice.

He rose up to his full height, turned slowly to study at each and every wolf surrounding the sacred circle. His chest expanded, life pouring through him, burning away his regrets in its path. His skin tingled the same as when his wolf wanted out.

He let his voice boom so everyone here would hear, filled with the sound of the alpha in him. "The reign of Ramsey Crescent is over. I claim the Crescent Bay pack as my own, and you shall henceforth be known as..." He glanced over at Zara and was inspired. "Serenity Bay, where we can all be at peace."

The majority of the wolves in the circle either bowed to him or lifted their voices in a howl to accept Niko as their new alpha. A few of them fled, including the asshole enforcer. That didn't surprise Niko at all. Ramsey may not have had his finger on the pulse of his pack, but he wouldn't have remained in power as long as he had without some supporters.

There were more one-bloods in the wolf world than he wanted to admit. The best means to combat that disgusting insurgency was to be an example of a better way. Niko reached his hand out for Zara and when she took it, he pulled her into the circle and kissed her for all of his new pack to see.

She smiled against his lips, swept her hands into his hair, and wrapped her ankle around the back of his leg like the sexy-ass siren she was. He reciprocated by dipping her and pinching her butt. She squeaked and he chuckled into her mouth. "You love it, and you know it.

"I do, but your shiny new pack doesn't need to see that."

"You do know when we have our mating ceremony, we'll be doing that and a whole lot more in front of all of them."

"Uh. I did not. No one said anything about public sex." She raised an eyebrow at him. "I guess I'd better get myself a fetish for being watched in the next couple of weeks."

She laughed, but then her smile faded, and Zara's eyes got that white glow to them when she was having a vision. Shit. She was so vulnerable during her trances. Before he could do anything, she was back locked eyes with him. "Someone is coming. Three men, who aren't men. Two in flowing gold robes with fur and jewels like some kind of royalty or something, but the other one looks like a homeless guy in an all black robe with a hood. They each have an enormous amount of power around them."

"The Volkovs." What the hell were they doing here? They never left Russia, or at least hadn't for at least a century.

Zara's eyes got wide. "Who? Wait, that's Mikhail's family?"

"Not exactly. He became a Volkov when he became Tzar. The Volkovs are, hmm, sort of hard to explain. They're like the Pope, but when the church had more influence hundreds of years ago. They choose who will lead all of wolfkind and confer on him the sovereignty of the Wolf Tzar." Niko had seen firsthand how their power and hunger corrupted them and all of wolfkind.

"They have become treacherous in their search for more influence in the past hundred years. But wolfkind is slow to change and many would not recognize the exploitation of our people. It is why my family and so many others left for America at the turn of the 18th century." That act by his grandfather had sparked a revolution of its own. Wolves around the world began integrating themselves into human society despite the wishes of the Volkovs.

That was the first time the *Streltsy* had stepped in to curtail the Volkovs' rule, led by Tsarina Sophia Alexseyevna, who happened to be Selena Troika's grandmother.

Revolution ran in their family.

"Why would you go to Russia and serve them?" Zara looked as though she'd eaten something sour.

It wasn't like wolfkind had history books for him to give to Zara so she could study up on wolf lore and traditions. No one had ever had to teach a human mate about why wolfkind was the way they were. "Even if I don't agree with the way they rule, I am still subservient to the commands of the Tzar. He is alpha of all, and all of wolfkind must do as he commands. Every pack is required to serve the Volkovs in some way. They maintain their power by making sure even the strongest of alphas understand who is really in charge. I was lucky that my family knew Mik's when we were kids, and he was able to conscript me into his personal guard. But even he was controlled by them. Until—I got there, and killed him."

She shook her head and frowned at him. "You didn't. That demon—"

One of the Crescent wolves stepped forward and interrupted, clearly worked up and worried about the Volkovs' invasion. "Sir. Should we assemble more enforcers? Make a stand?"

Niko swallowed hard and stared at Zara. Demon. She'd specifically said the word demon. It took him a minute to realize the enforcer was standing there waiting on a response from him. "We cannot fight them."

He wasn't sure if he was talking about the Volkovs or demons. Maybe they were one and the same.

The enforcer didn't like that answer. "You'll just allow them to destroy us?"

"No, I will not." Niko finally tore his eyes from Zara's and looked around the clearing at his new pack. His people. That he would defend from the machinations of the Volkovs at all costs. "You know your hierarchy here better than I do. Choose some strong enforcers to gather the women and children, including the human women Ramsey has been holding here, and take them to Troika territory. Selena will receive you, and my brothers will protect everyone."

Zara quirked her head to the side and the white light filled her eyes, but only for a brief moment. She blinked and shook her head. "They're here... and so are your brothers."

Fuck a duck.

From the darkest shadows on the far side of the sacred circle, three somber figures emerged. Two that Niko recognized dressed in gold robes and a third he didn't know in black, just as Zara said. From the other side, Max and Galyna appeared in their wolf forms, followed by Kosta and Heli as humans.

Max spoke into his head. *Told you three heads were better than one. I'm gonna assume you can't fucking count, because I know you wouldn't face the Volkovs without your family.*

Kosta nodded and glanced over at the imposing trio moving across the circle toward them. "We're here for you, brother. We stand with you, until the end if needs be."

Dumuzid Volkov stepped forward to the head of the triad and slowly clapped his hands. "I see congratulations are in order, Nikolai. Well done destroying your enemy and winning back the loyalty of your brothers. We weren't sure you had it in you. But you have truly demonstrated that you are indeed an alpha among alphas."

Max lowered his snout and growled. *Niko never lost our allegiance, the Volkovs and their tyranny have.*

Dumuzid glanced over at the other golden robed specter, Grigori Yefimovich Volkov. Better known as Rasputin.

He was the eldest Volkov, and likely the oldest living wolf, despite the rumors he'd been killed along with the Romanovs whom he had so much influence over all those years ago. Grigori and Dumuzid communicated something in that look which Niko could tell was going to spell trouble.

Dumuzid smiled and spread his arms, palms up in a gesture meant to be a platitude. "Will you still find us tyrannous, little brother, when we declare your Nikolai is our new Wolf Tzar?"

DEMONS STINK

Zara watched the trio of Volkovs closely. The power emanating off of them made her skin itch. When she glanced around at the circle, most of the people and wolves were staring, a bit slack jawed. She understood how they felt. There was something not right about that Dumuzid guy.

She listened to the interaction between them and Niko as she inched her way toward Heli. She whispered as quietly as she could. "Can you see anything?"

"Yeah. I see some serious asses who are going to get their holes kicked by my honey bunny in a minute." Heli made a face at the Volkovs and then a blew a kiss to Kosta.

"No, you goober." Sigh. Little sisters. Eye roll. "I mean visions. Do you see what's about to happen?"

"It's the weirdest thing. I keep getting flashes like I'm about to get a flash of insight and then it kind of fritzes out. I think one of those dudes is doing something to interfere with my power, yo."

Zara didn't need a vision to know that life-changing

events were about to happen. There was almost an electrical surge in the air. The stench of tainted smoke floated around them and... weird... was that what brimstone smelled like?

Crap on a cracker. That's probably what a freaking monster from hell wreaked of. The guy in the black cape and hood hadn't revealed himself yet. They couldn't see his face or his eyes or anything. "I think that guy in the black robe is a demon."

Galyna's voice popped into her head. *Like a dementor?*

"Worse." Zara didn't know if Dumuzid was controlling the demon or if the demon had command over the wolf Pope dudes. Either was bad. Now would be another great time for a vision of her own.

Heli grimaced. "Okay. Shitbuckets. What are we going to do?

I didn't think to bring freaking chocolate frogs with me. Our Defense Against the Dark Arts isn't advanced enough for a battle against minions of the Voldemortkovs.

If only she had some control over her stupid visions. She had to do something but what? "I'm going to try to-"

A force hit Zara in the face. She grabbed at her temples as if she could hold whatever it was at bay. It felt like insects were drilling into her brain and telling her to kneel down. Dumuzid smiled and spread his arms, palms up in a fake gesture she'd seen skeevy lawyers do when they were trying to play to the jury like they were friends. "Will you still find us tyrannous, little brother, when we declare your Nikolai as our new Wolf Tzar?"

Zara's world tilted and went white. She tried to breathe and inhaled gauzy white material. She coughed and pulled her face off the sleeve of the woman in white.

There you go, you got it. Sorry for sucking you into the vision like that, but you got distracted.

"Where are we?"

Neither here nor there. It's important you see this quickly though, so quit gabbing with me and see what you need to see.

Zara gaped at the woman. The woman closed her mouth with a knuckle under her chin, and then turned her head to the side. Niko was standing on a snowy hilltop, golden robes around him and black holes where his eyes should be.

"Niko," she shouted.

He can't hear you. He's not here... yet.

Dumuzid appeared behind Niko's shoulder and set his hand on him. A mass of black creatures that looked like a cross between snakes, men, and ostriches, with a dash of bat thrown in, poured out of their shadows. They were followed by a crone woman dressed all in black who rose up on a black plume of smoke.

No wait. That wasn't smoke. It was a dragon. An enormous black, scary-as-all-get-out, dragon with red glowing eyes. The demon... A demon dragon.

The crone patted Dumuzid on the shoulder as if telling him he'd done a good job. He smiled and held out his arms to a woman who appeared out of the shadows behind the crone. "Brother? You've done it. You've saved me from Inanna's punishment."

The woman ran to her brother and kissed him on the lips...passionately.

Eww. If Zara was lucky and this was anything like Game of Thrones, spoiler alert, things would not end well for incestuous siblings. Blech. Also, that dragon would rain fire down on the whole lot of them.

Alongside the trio of grossness, Niko snarled and shifted into his gorgeous white wolf. His fur was streaked with wide swaths of red blood. He howled and legions of wolves joined the ranks of the snake dudes.

"What are they all gathering to do? It looks like they're about to go to war."

"Look." The woman pointed down the hill where people, including her mother and father, were gathered. They were fenced in, like cattle in a stockyard and all around them her precious little town of Rogue was on fire.

"Oh my God." Before the words were even out of her mouth the wolves and snake men charged toward the trapped humans. The people screamed and Zara gulped for air, her heart skipped so many beats it may have stopped, and tears pooled in her eyes. "Make it stop. Make it stop."

The vision faded and the sounds muted, but the attack continued. *I can't make it stop. But you can. End this alliance before it ever starts and change the future. Give my sons a chance to defeat evil.*

Good versus evil? This was so far beyond the scope of what she'd set out to do when she wanted to take down Crescent, and happened to fall back in love with Niko. Now she had to stop a war between heaven and hell too? "How? Just tell me what to do and I'll do it."

She had a horrible feeling this was going to hurt.

Love. That's what all of this is about. The answer is always love.

Zara's eyes snapped open and she was back in the sacred circle. She grumbled under her breath. "Are you freaking kidding me?"

What the hell was she supposed to do with that answer? She already loved Niko, he knew that. She'd told him so just earlier today. Hadn't she? Shoot. Now she wasn't sure. Surely, she had. He'd said it to her.

"Kneel, Nikolai Piotryvich Troika and accept your place as Tzar of the wolves." Dumuzid pointed to the ground in front of Niko.

Oh no. Niko couldn't be Tzar, that was the beginning of the end for them all. "Niko, no."

Zara rushed forward, shoving people and wolves out of her way. It was then that she noticed almost everyone was frozen, down on their knees and staring straight ahead at Niko and the Volkovs. Except for her. She slowed and stared around her.

Heli and Kosta were still standing but were struggling to move. Gal and Max were very, very slowly stalking forward as if they were having to wade through quicksand made of cement surrounded in glue.

"Kneel, Zarenity, daughter of no wolf, and become Tsarina at your master's side." Dumuzid pointed at her, and she half expected rays of colorful magic or lightning to come flying out of his fingers.

That same itchy power that struck at her before, hit her again. Her knees wobbled, but she did not fall. She had to get to Niko and make sure he knew she loved him. "You have no control over me, slave to a demon. I know your secret. I have seen the future."

"You know nothing," he spat. "Slave? You are mistaken. Only weak wolves fall prey to demons."

"Zara," Niko's voice cracked on her name, and he reached his arm out for her.

That buoyed her like the best lifeline. The people around her, that she loved the absolute most in her life, were the ones resisting this manipulative prickhole's crazy-ass powers.

The power of love... Amazeballs.

Zara made her way to Niko and gripped his hand in hers. Warmth curled through her from his touch. The stiffness in Niko's body released, and he had control over himself again.

"You've overstepped your purview Volkov and failed. The reign of your Tzars are over. I will not be your puppet." Niko's words rang with power, and his eyes glowed so brightly the whole sacred circle filled with the amber light, pouring from him and every wolf around them.

"My reach is farther than even you can imagine, wolf. You will be the Wolf Tzar and do as we command, or an army of demons will destroy all of the Crescents, the Troikas, Zara, and her family. Do you want that on your conscience? I don't think your soul can handle much more guilt... Can it?"

Niko squeezed Zara's hand so tight it was painful. But there was no way she was letting him go. "Niko has nothing to be guilty about."

"Really? Killing his best friend, allowing wolfkind fall into chaos without a clear leader, and starting a pack war, aren't offenses dark enough to keep him awake at night? Even his own wolf has deserted him, hasn't it?" Dumuzid needled them both with his accusations.

Zara knew better. "Niko did none of those things."

"*Solnyshka,* I love that you believe in me so deeply. But I did all of that, and my soul is indeed black for it." Niko's voice wavered, breaking her heart. "You have already seen that I cannot shift into my wolf form. There is too much truth in what he says. I will never be his puppet, but I am also not worthy to rule my people."

"You're right about one thing. I do believe in you deeply, and just in case I didn't say it before because I was overly distracted by orgasms, I love you."

"Enough," Dumuzid groaned. "Kneel before me or face my wrath."

Zara stood up on her tippy-toes and kissed Niko on the side of his mouth. "I got you, wolf of mine. Believe in me, like I believe in you."

She faced Dumuzid and pointed at his dirty, tainted heart. "Niko tried to save Mikhail. The two of them saw through your façade. You're not even a wolf and have no rights over them. You and your demon master killed Mikhail. I saw your act of treason, and I bear witness. Release his memories... Now."

Dumuzid narrowed his eyes and directed a whole new wave of power at her. Zara felt his compulsion, which was also filled with a dark lust and a craving for blood. Whatever kind of creature he was, he had some serious issues. She didn't even bend a little under his push. He crowed his frustration with her and stalked forward.

Niko stepped between them. His arms and shoulders expanded, fur sprouted from his skin, and he looked distinctly werewolf-ish. Scary. "Don't even think about touching my mate. Do as she says and let me see the truth of what happened to Mik."

Dumuzid glanced at his compatriot in the black cape. The man, who Zara assumed was a demon, threw off his cloak and black wings spread from his back. He lowered his head and growled at them, smoke and fire pouring from his mouth and nostrils. His transformation continued, black and red magic swirling around him until his entire body shifted into that of a huge, honking, fire-breathing, black-scaled, dragon.

Zara stared into the eyes of the dragon and recognized that it too was being manipulated by whatever power Dumuzid had over most everyone in the sacred circle. Well, crap. That wasn't fair. Zara didn't think dragons were going to show up yet. Hopefully that creepy crone-witch-lady and the snake-bat-ostrich-men wouldn't pop up too. But they couldn't count on it.

"You see, I am no slave to a demon, but you will be." Dumuzid threw his golden cloaks off and the wrinkles of his old decrepit face faded away. He transformed into a suave-looking ladies' man, dressed in a black suit and slicked back hair. "Nor am I a wolf. Although, it wasn't hard to penetrate their ranks as if I was. Their minds are so easily manipulated."

Ooh, that was a low blow. She had a retort on her lips, but Niko beat her to the punch. "Because you haven't allowed us to fall in love with our true mates. You've kept us from our destinies and suppressed my people for far too long. Your reign is over. Now."

Zara poked her head out from behind Niko's hulked-out form which she could no longer see around. "Yeah, assmunch."

"I've had enough of your smart-mouth, you fat bitch. I don't need you to win this war, only the Tzar."

Dumuzid waved his dragon forward. "Eat her."

FIGHT, FIGHT, FIGHT

$\mathcal{N}$iko shoved Zara out of the way of the charging dragon and jumped on the beast's head. He still didn't have his wolf or it's deadly power, but his claws were enough to kill Ramsey Crescent, they would at least act as a painful distraction for Dumuzid's guard dragon. He sunk his claws under the dragon's scales and pierced his skin.

The dragon roared and thrashed about trying to get Niko off, but it was holding back. The poor beast was under Dumuzid's control too, so Niko wouldn't kill it. He understood better than most what that was like, now that he had his memories back and they fueled his rage.

The second Zara revealed the truth, he didn't even need her to tell the bastard to release the block in his mind. He saw the whole scene as clear as the night it had happened. His heart ached at the death of his friend, but without the taint of guilt that had shrouded him for so long.

His true mate once again found a way to heal him and set him free.

He and Mik had fought Dumuzid and some kind of

horrible snake-like demons side by side. He hadn't murdered his best friend. Mikhail died a warrior's death, taking a claw to the heart and throat. Not something even their healing abilities could overcome.

Niko would not allow Dumuzid to do that to anyone else ever again, even if that meant showing mercy to his enemy. "Fight his control, dragon. You do not have to do his bidding. Attack him, not me."

The beast flailed and screeched out a horrible bellow. It thrashed and threw Niko to the ground, then stalked toward him, teeth bared, and he trapped Niko beneath his giant talons. *I do as the witch's servant wants because it will get me what I need. Your soul was once empty too, wolf.*

A soulless dragon was a dangerous foe. But Niko didn't believe the beast had nothing in his heart. He could see the battle warring between good and evil, right and wrong in the dragon's black eyes. Niko recognized all that because he saw himself reflected there. This dragon hated what he was and wanted something better.

"Dumuzid and his brethren can't give you what you want. You need to find yourself a mate."

The dragon growled and squeezed Niko's chest to the point of asphyxiation. His ribs cracked.

No soul. No mate.

He couldn't speak, much less breath to refute the brute's false belief.

Zara screamed and they both looked over to see what was happening. That break in the battle gave Niko the chance to roll out from the beast's claws and make a run for his mate. He couldn't allow the bastard to harm his one true love and destroy everything. He would save her this time.

Dumuzid gripped Zara's arms and was trying to drag her away. He had fangs that were nothing like a wolf's and they were dripping with saliva. "You're more trouble than you're worth. I'm going to enjoy drinking every last drop of your blood, even if it will probably go straight to my waist since you're so fucking fat."

"Get your hands off me, you fat-shaming demon spawn." She slapped his face and left three lines of claw marks across his cheek.

Claw marks.

They'd told him marked humans either got psychic powers or the ability to shift into wolves. Could Zara have both? If she was a wolf, and he was her master, he could use his alpha voice to make her shift. It was worth a shot if it would save her.

He sprinted across the circle toward her and pulled every bit of power he had, pushing it out in his alpha voice. "Shift Zara. I command you."

All eyes turned on him, Dumuzid's wide with surprise then glanced at Zara as if he thought she'd turn into a dirty snot rag instead of a wolf.

Zara didn't shift. She did however use the distraction to knee her captor in the groin. The jackass went down with a groan.

Either Zara did have some supernatural strength or Dumuzid was particularly vulnerable. It was never pleasant for any dude to get kneed in the junk, but a human female wouldn't be able to do much damage to a shifter.

But Dumuzid wasn't a wolf. Realization hit Niko in the gut like a cannonball. Well, holy shit. Drinks blood, sensitive manhood, power to compel. It all added up to only one thing.

He was an incubus. Those demons had dicks practically made of glass.

Rasputin hadn't moved once since this battle had started. He simply stared at Niko like he was the most interesting character on a TV show. "You cannot use your alpha voice on her, *malenky tsar*, but you can use it on your pack. You are their leader after all."

Niko would like to rail at Rasputin for allowing a demon among the Volkov, for not doing anything to stop this abomination, but that would have to wait, because that was actually a good fucking point. Maybe being an ancient Volkov had its advantages.

Since Zara had taken care of Dumuzid for the moment, Niko pivoted and faced the majority of the people and wolves standing on one side of the sacred circle. They were all frozen in place by the incubus's compulsion except for his brothers and their mates who had some control over their own bodies. Niko didn't know if his alpha voice would still work on Max and Kosta now that he had a pack, and they weren't in it. It definitely wouldn't work on Heli or Galyna, but some back up was better than none and he had to try.

From somewhere deep inside, Niko pulled once again on the power that made him an alpha, the same one that Zara had healed in him with her love and belief that he was a good man. He let it rise up his throat and howled with the strength of a thousand wolves. "Awaken, wolves. Shift into your true forms."

Niko felt his own body, his bones, muscles, and skin change. With every pop, stretch, and tear of skin, he praised the Goddess and his true love for helping him find what made him who he truly was. Niko landed on all fours and scratched at the ground beneath his paws. He growled, let out a resounding bark, and lifted his face to the moonless sky in another howl filled with gratitude, hope, and the promise of vengeance.

For the first time since Mik's death, Niko was once again, the great white wolf.

He faced his pack and spoke into their minds with the dominance of not only his alpha voice but all the alphas before him. *Join the battle to save our kind from the evil ploy of hell to infiltrate our proud race and tear us apart from the inside. Awaken and fight alongside me.*

The weight and authority rang through with such power that his howl shook the leaves off the trees and swept through the people gathered around like an earthquake. Every person fell to their hands and knees and became wolves in every color of nature's rainbow.

Even Heli, who hadn't manifested the ability to shift, changed into a plush tawny wolf, the same as her soft wheat-colored hair. Kosta in his wolf form stared at her with a purple glow in his eyes, and Heli's matched with her own lavender gleam.

Max and Galyna were already in their wolf forms, but on his command, their eyes glowed with the Troika blue that all the wolves of their combined packs had. The same hot fiery blue Niko and Kosta had grown up with.

Now with their own packs, their eyes had transformed into that of their true selves, of the alphas they were all meant to be.

Niko glanced around at the Serenity Bay wolves and they returned his appraisal with incandescent eyes of amber flames. The color he'd seen in the mirror when he and Zara

were together. They showed him their deference and acceptance as their leader by turning their heads and showing their
throats to him as was his people's way.

Niko vowed to be the best ruler he could be for them.

*Enforcers. Surround the incubus and the dragon. But do not
harm them. I want them both alive.* He waited until the mass of
enforcers moved in, closing their ranks on their common
enemy. Niko lowered his head almost to the ground, until he
was just about eye level with Dumuzid. *The right to kill the
demon for his crimes is mine alone.*

The enforcers including Max and Kosta formed a growling, snarling circle around the demon and his dragon. The
dragon did nothing to resist, except a few swipes of his spiked
tail to warn the wolves behind him from getting too close.

Dumuzid slowly got back to his feet and glared at Niko.
"You will never–"

"Shut up." Zara pointed a finger at Dumuzid and dropped
her gaze to his crotch. He shut up.

Niko stalked forward ready to pounce on the bastard if he
had to. Yes, he wanted to question Dumuzid to find out how
this whole plot to infiltrate the Volkovs happened and how
long it had been going on, but he'd be perfectly happy not
knowing anything if Dumuzid moved a single muscle toward
Zara. He didn't like her being that close to the demon, but he
loved her strength and bravery even more.

Niko fired his questions off and stalked around the false
Volkov in slow circles with his teeth bared and tail swishing
back and forth menacingly. *How long has this been going on,
incubus? Why have you infiltrated the wolf community? How does
that benefit you and your kind?*

Dumuzid stayed staunchly quiet and glared back at Niko.

Rasputin didn't however. He too had shifted into his wolf form on Niko's command. He stretched and shifted back into a human and stepped into the circle of enforcers. "We all have things we want. Some of us make deals with devils to get what we crave."

He shrugged like that was no big deal. "You assume it's for power and influence, but it rarely is. I did it to be with the woman I loved."

Holy shit? Rasputin in love was an unsettling thought.

"She was human. Not just any peasant, but royalty. The centuries of wars against wolves made our ban on mating outside the species a must. Not a law easily broken. So, I made a deal so I could be with my Alexandra."

His shoulders sagged. "We all know how that tragic story ends. Poor little Anastasia alone escaped."

Zara looked at Niko and gave him is-he-kidding-me eyes. He nodded back at her. He was as shocked as she was that a Volkov, one of the wolves who made the rules, would break their most rigid edict. *Yes, solnyshka, I do believe he is referring to the Romanovs.*

Rasputin didn't take any notice. "None of that would have been necessary if the Volkov's would have lifted the ban on interracial mating when I asked them to. The next hundred years would have been very different for both wolfkind and humans if they had."

Huh. Rasputin, the corrupt mystic and powerful Volkov wolf was on their side? That was too weird to comprehend. Niko didn't trust the implication.

"Why didn't you change the laws, you schmoe? You're one of these all powerful Volkovs, you could have used your influence for good, dammit." Zara's voice was filled with so much disdain, it was almost funny. His fiery mate was going to eviscerate Grigori Rasputin.

"It's not that simple," he said with an almost sad forlorn quality.

Niko refused to feel sorry for Rasputin and the misguided decisions he'd made. Zara was right. He could have changed everything. Mik might not have had to die if he had. In Niko's eyes, that made him as guilty as Dumuzid.

Zara threw her hands in the air. "Yeah it is. You simply say, hey wolfkind, mate whoever the hell you want. Have fun."

"Don't be stupid. Wolves need a tight rein or they run amok. We tried your way in the sixteen-hundreds. Just look at how many mates were burned at the stake as witches. Mankind will never understand anything beyond their banal beliefs. Which is why you must be eliminated and end wolfkind's temptation for your sins of the flesh." Rasputin's eyes glowed, not with the intensity of his wolf, but with a dark power fueled by hatred.

He waved Zara away dismissively, and focused his death glare in on Niko. "You, on the other hand, have the ability be a great leader and take our kind into that future where we rule over the land and beasts alike. We'll just have to remove any distractions you have first, so you can become the most powerful Tzar of the Wolves in our history."

Niko didn't even have a chance to react to Rasputin words before he nodded at Dumuzid who sneered and sent out a wave of his compulsion. Niko withstood the flash of possession like nothing more than a stiff wind blowing through his fur. "Good try, demon. Your powers are useless against me now."

That pissed the incubus off. "Let's see how you feel once

you and your love are separated by the seven gates of Hell, wolf." Dumuzid jumped forward and snagged Zara around the throat, sinking his fangs into her throat.

Niko roared and leaped through the air to destroy this enemy once and for all. His heart squeezed in his chest even though he begged it to give him the rush of blood and adrenaline he needed to power his muscles. His teeth and claws hit the hard scales of the black dragon's armor as it lashed out at him, protecting the incubus. When Niko bit down to sever the beast's tail from his body, the dragon disappeared along with Dumuzid and Zara, leaving Niko's mouth full of nothing but shadows and smoke.

"Now that's done, come bow before me and receive the blessing of the Volkovs, Tzar Nikolai."

Niko turned on Rasputin and swiped his great claws across the man's throat, severing his head from his body, letting the spray of red soak into his white fur, covering him in the blood of his foes.

He would wear that symbol of war until he was reunited with Zara. If Zara died, all the wolves under his rule would wear the blood of their enemies for all time, because Niko would burn down the world.

LIVE AND LEARN IN HELL

Zara landed on her hands and knees on a hard dirt and rock floor, scraping a thousand tiny cuts into her skin on the jagged stones. Then she promptly threw up. On Dumuzid's shoes.

"You humans are disgusting." He grabbed her by the shoulder, digging his craggy nails into her, and yanked her up. "Come on. We might as well get this over with."

She did not enjoy being manhandled, but she couldn't seem to make her feet go under her either. She'd tell him to fuck off and let go of her in a second. Just as soon as she caught her breath and stopped feeling like she was going to fall face first into a lake of boiling lava.

Oh shit. That really was a huge pool of molten rock he was dragging her past. The place stank of sulfur and dead things. "Where are we? How did we get here?"

And where was Niko? She'd seen him attack in his great white wolf form, but then everything had gone dark. Her stomach roiled again at even the hint of a thought that he could be....

Bile rose up her throat. Bu-uurp. Nope. Not going there. Niko was fine… Fine. She was going to figure out a way to get back to him. He was probably worried out of his skull.

The black dragon was a few feet ahead of them and a shimmer of something sparkly swirled around his great scaly body. In a blink, he was a man, fully dressed in jeans and a t-shirt, but no shoes and jet-black hair that had definitely never seen a barber, or a bar of soap. "Welcome to Hell."

Wait… Literally? If this was the domain of the devil, where were all the lawyers? Her face must have telegraphed her thoughts, because the dragon guy smirked. He wasn't making a friendly overture by any means, but there was a quality in his black gaze that was vaguely familiar.

Whoa. He had that same exact look that Niko had before they'd pledged their love for each other. It didn't take psychic abilities or even a degree in psychology to see that he had a deep hatred of who he was and desperately wanted to find a way to change that dark part of himself.

That meant he wasn't all bad. There was good in him and she was going to tap into that to get the hell out of Hell.

"Where are you taking me?" This time she addressed her question to the dragon guy.

Dumuzid shoved her. "Don't talk to the demon dragons unless you want your eyeballs scratched out."

His words were more than a mere warning. There was a compulsion in them she hadn't felt before. She was sure she was supposed to feel lust and the will to obey what he was saying, but it was like there was a strange shield between his words and their intentions. "Never mind, chat the whole lot of the stupid bastards up. I would enjoy seeing that."

"Why don't you go hang out with them, sicko." She gave him the finger and waited for the inevitable fat slam.

Dumuzid looked around the cavern and found a group of snakey dudes. Oh, there were the lawyers. He signaled them to come over. "Hey there, fellow demons, how's tricks?"

The snake-bat things growled and bared very stinky teeth at him. They hissed at both of them and flapped their wings until the black dragon guy shooed them away. "What the fuck are you doing, demon? Stay away from my brethren. They are not your playthings."

Okay. Zara had gotten used to the abnormal being the norm in the past few days and had even accepted that what she'd previously thought was a mental illness might be a superpower, but her mind said, that's enough crazeballs, time to analyze this situation with logic.

There were a couple of really weird things that happened a moment ago. A. Dumuzid didn't seem like he was screwing around. He'd done what she told him to without even realizing it. And B. The snake dudes were the dragon guy's family? Hell was a seriously wack-a-doo place.

She could use this bizarro information to escape. Somehow. Her brain raced to process everything happening around her and fit it into the puzzle.

Dumuzid backed away from both the snake creatures and their big brother dragon guy. He turned on her and glared, looking her up and down like he could find some magical mind control power. "Kneel before me."

Zara frowned at him. "Are you talking to me? If you are, no thanks. I've already got rocks embedded in my kneecaps. You kneel."

Dumuzid sank to his knees and then flipped his shit. "How

are you doing this, witch? I bit you, I tasted your blood in my mouth and bonded you to me. You must do as I say."

Ha ha. This was rich. She might not know where she was or if Niko was okay, but she was not going to be afraid of this asshat ever again. "I think your blood bond thingy backfired, dumb ass. Now get me out of here and back to my mate."

The black dragon guy laughed, but then his face changed to an expression of extreme disdain and even anger. He said, "Too late. The King of Hell is here."

Zara looked up from her demon minion to see a really, really, really big black dragon stomp into the cavern, spy them, and roar so loudly, stalactites dropped from the ceiling like rock daggers. She probably should have dived for cover, but that whole flight-or-fight response thing in her must be broken because she completely froze.

The dragon stalked toward their little group and transformed into a giant of a man, mid-stride. He grabbed Dumuzid by his shirt, dragging him up from the ground and shook the little bastard like a rag doll. "What the fuck are you doing here, incubus?"

"I...I've brought you the mate of the Wolf Tzar."

The King of Hell glared at Dumuzid and then glanced over at Zara. She blinked and still couldn't move. Come on legs, what the heck was wrong with her? She needed to run, to flee. Right now. She was probably going to be murdered right here and that sucked big scaly balls. She didn't want to die. She wanted to be with Niko and have his babies or wolf pups or whatever. She willed her legs to go and finally managed to take a step back.

"You mean, you ran at the first sign of a fight, you filthy coward. I should have known better than to send a shepherd in place of a warrior." The man dropped Dumuzid and walked over to her. He looked her up and down and then he sniffed her, getting up all into her business.

Blech. She felt like Sigourney Weaver in Alien, just waiting for him to drip slobber on her. "She is not a dragon's mate. She has no soul shard. What the fuck am I supposed to do with her, give her to the Annunaki as a plaything?"

Dumuzid reached up from his permanent position licking the King of Hell's boots. "You can use her as a negotiation tool."

"You're my negotiation tool, fucker. If the two of you being here with her in tow means you haven't turned the new Tzar, and he and his wolves won't be joining the ranks of my army, your immortality is over. Winter is coming. Crone," he shouted for someone.

The creepiest looking old lady in black tattered robes hobbled her way into the cavern. What the shit? Now it all made sense. The dragon, the crone, wanting Niko to join their army. She was seeing everything leading up to her vision, her prophecy that the world was going to end under the rule of paranormal beasts' rule.

The crone examined Zara and it felt like a million ants were crawling through her head. Before she could scream, it stopped and the crone spoke to the King. "She could still be useful to us. Her mind is filled with my sister's magic."

"No, I'm not wasting any more time on your plots, witch." The King pointed at the dragon dude Zara had hoped might be on her team. "You, get rid of her."

Dragon guy grabbed her arm and dragged her towards the far side of the cavern where the crone had come from. She was really damn sick of people grabbing her and dragging her around. At least this time it was out of danger. Hopefully not out of the frying pan and into the fire. It's not like she knew where he was taking her.

The King of Hell continued to berate Dumuzid, and Zara listened with half an ear in case she heard something that would be useful to help her escape.

"You've failed me, Dumuzid and your time on Earth is almost up. You and your sister couldn't fulfill your promises. Have fun roasting in my little corner of hell together while the mortal plane freezes over."

"No... Wait." Dumuzid whimpered. "Geshtianna has another way."

Zara whispered to dragon dude. "Can you help me get out of here?"

"Why would I do that? I'm already on his shit list." He shoved his thumb over his shoulder in the King's direction.

A woman appeared at the entrance to the cavern. She was just as dirty as dragon guy but dressed all in red leather and had about a dozen daggers hanging from various spots on her outfit. "Because, Jett... She can see."

Jett, formerly known as dragon dude, stopped in his tracks and Zara almost tumbled over. Apparently, he understood what the lady in red meant. "Can you see how to defeat him?"

Her visions. Crap. "They don't work like that, I don't just make them appear."

He glared at her and bared his teeth. The blackness swirled in his eyes. "Then I have no reason to help you."

The lady in red pulled out a dagger and held it to Jett's throat. "Go away."

The knife to his jugular didn't seem to faze Jett. He rolled his eyes at this woman. "Fine."

He looked over at Zara and dipped his head at the lady. "Good luck with that."

He moved about three feet away and leaned against the wall as if it was a comfortable place to hang out and watch Dumuzid get thrown into the lake of lava, which was Zara's guess about what was going to happen.

The lady in red grabbed Zara's shirt and squatted down to watch too, indicating Zara should join her. She'd rather leave, but it wasn't like she knew where to go.

The King roared. "I'm finished with you both. Inanna's punishment stands. I will send my own demons to find me a soul shard."

Dumuzid scrambled away. "Give us one more chance. There is a succubus who has the gift of the dragon's daughter in her. One of Leonard's offspring. She will be able to use her glamour and get a shard. From a Wyvern."

The King stared at Dumuzid for way longer than was comfortable, then sighed and looked at the crone. "Is this true? A succubus dragon's daughter?"

The crone's eyes turned black and she stared off into space. Gah. Was that what Zara looked like when she got a vision? "Yes. But their bloodline protects them from my sight. I cannot see her clearly. Call the red daughter in, she will be able to hear the dragon's daughter."

The lady in red pulled more daggers out of her shirt and held them all pointed at the Crone. She was the King's daughter? This place was one fucked up dysfunctional family.

"You leave Fallyn out of this." The King spat and turned back to Dumuzid. "You know who this succubus is?"

"Yes." The incubus nodded quickly. "Geshtianna can command her to serve. She'll be able to take the shard."

"Fool." The king smacked Dumuzid across the face sending him flying way too close to the lava. Zara couldn't say she didn't root for him to tumble in and get his bones melted. He skidded to a stop and the King stalked toward him. "A shard can only be given. If she is a dragon's daughter, she will not want to give it up except to her mate."

The King glanced around the cavern and pointed at dragon dude. "Take Jett to Geshtianna's coven. Make this succubus think he is her mate, but they can't be together until she finds him a shard."

"Fuck me." Jett whispered under his breath.

"Yes, sire." Dumuzid clambered to his feet and rushed over to Jett, probably pretty damn anxious to leave on his new mission.

If Zara got out of here in one piece, she needed to remember as much of this scenario as she could and try to warn the dragons. Did she really just think that? An hour ago, she didn't even know these mythical creatures existed. Maybe they were enemies of the wolves. She'd have to ask Niko.

She refused to believe that she wouldn't see him again. She would, and they'd laugh and laugh about her adventures in hell. Someday.

"I warn you, I am sending my Galla demons to find a shard for myself. If they achieve their goal before yours, neither you nor your sister will ever see each other again." The King pointed to Dumuzid and then spit fire at him.

Dumuzid jumped away from the flames and toward Jett. "Get us out of here."

Jett rolled his eyes, which seemed to be his default expression when dealing with everyone from hell. "Where to, oh desperate one?"

"Emirates Palace, Abu Dhabi."

Zara whispered to Fallyn. "Is he speaking English?"

"Come on. Let's go before Kur-Jara notices us." She scooted into a dark tunnel and Zara followed.

Because what else was she going to do? Around a couple more corners and just when Zara was sure she'd gone blind because it had grown so dark, a light appeared in what looked like a small grotto. Fallyn walked into the cave-like space, but Zara took a moment to stare.

Hanging from every available space were thousands and thousands of shiny Christmas ornaments. Fallyn noticed Zara staring. "Don't touch them. They're mine."

Zara raised her palms to show evidence of keeping her hands off. Fallyn nodded and waved her in. Zara had to pass through what almost seemed like a curtain of sparkles, but that tingled when it touched her skin.

"Ereshkigal can't see in here." Fallyn tipped her head to the side and said, "You're not in my mind."

"Umm, no? Are you in mine? I have been known to hallucinate and this seems a lot like some of my head trips." She thought she could tell the difference now, but her last couple of visions had been awfully real. Maybe this hell place was a hallucination too.

"I can't hear you." The lady tapped her head.

It was pretty dang quiet in here. "I can talk louder."

"You don't belong here."

"I know. It's not as if I want to be here. Can you help me get home?" She was starting to feel like Dorothy in Oz. She'd definitely met the wicked witch and the wizard. Not sure if Jett was the scarecrow or the tin man, but Dumuzid was for sure the cowardly lion. If Fallyn told her to tap her heels together three times, Zara was checking herself back into the mental hospital.

Fallyn did not even notice Zara's shoes. She touched one of the shining ornaments that was painted with a quaint snowy scene. "Stop thinking with your eyes."

"I don't know what that means." Now she kind of wished the lady would give her something easy like chanting there's no place like home.

"Think with your sight." Fallyn opened her eyes wide. She reached forward and tapped Zara's temple. "What do you see?"

It was worth a try. Zara closed her eyes and a vision started right away. She was in a house, in a nursery, at night. There were two bassinets. "Babies. Twins."

"What kind of babies?"

Umm. "The baby kind?"

"Dragon babies?" Fallyn's voice was more excited than before. "Is her spell broken?"

Zara moved closer. Two sweet adorable faces were sleeping peacefully. They each had a stuffed dog in the crib with them. One with its head ripped half off. "They definitely aren't dragons."

Didn't dragons hatch from eggs? They did on TV and in books. This was real life though and someday, she was making Galyna help her write a fricking beginners guide to the paranormal, so other women who mated wolves, or dragons for that matter would know what the heck people were on about all the time.

The lady harrumphed. "What are their names?"

Zara looked around the nursery which was decorated in a nature theme with trees that reminded her of home. Over each of the bassinets was a little plaque with a name printed in beautiful calligraphy. "I see something, but their names are kind of hard to read."

"You can read?" She said it like she couldn't.

Maybe Zara could get her into a literacy program in Rogue or Cape Cod. "Yes. Her name is Eleanor."

The vision ended and Zara opened her eyes. She had to blink a few times and then realized those weren't spots in her vision, it was more Christmas balls.

The woman tipped her head to the side as if she was hearing something else.

"What is it? Is the King coming? More of those snake-men?" She shouldn't be screwing around thinking about babies when she needed to figure out how to escape.

"Shh." Fallyn waved Zara off like a buzzing fly. "I can't hear her if you're talking to me. No, not you, Izzy. You're sure? That's her. No, I can't go. Fine. I'll ask. What's the boy's name?"

Zara pointed to herself. "Wait, me? Are you talking to me?"

"Yes," she said impatiently. "What's his name."

"Who?"

"The baby."

When Zara saw they were twins, she assumed they would be identical. But the woman was correct now that she thought about what she'd seen. The other baby was a boy. She squinted in her mind's eye to see the name tag above his head. "Tristan."

The lady pursed her lips and nodded. "How ironic."

"It is?"

"Yes. You'll see. You should go now. Ereshkigal wants to touch your brains." The lady led Zara to the other side of her

Christmas ornament hoard, to a pile of swords, knives, and various and sundry weaponry straight out of medieval armories. "There. This is my shadow. It will take you where you want to go."

Travel by shadow. Why not? "Thank you. Can you come with me? Do you have to go back to that place?"

Fallyn shook her head. "I still have to save the mermaid."

That did it. This was now officially the weirdest conversation she'd ever had.

"I had an auntie like you once. Tante Inanna. I liked her. She gave me pretty shiny things. You should give Ellie pretty shiny things.

Auntie. Ellie. She was telling Zara those babies were her niece and nephew. Wait till she told Heli and Galyna. Oh... Galyna. They were going to be Gal's children. Zara glanced around at the ornaments and the highly polished weapons. They seemed like strange presents, but those knives and things could come in handy for a young girl who would someday grow up to be a warrior. "I will do that. I promise you."

"Good. Then I give you the gift of a clear mind. Give your memories to me. You shall not remember this place or what happened here." The woman tapped the center of Zara's forehead.

A supernova erupted behind her eyes, blinding her with a white light. She had the distinct feeling that strings were being pulled out of her head and being wound up into someone else's brain. Spots swam around her eyes and through them she could just make out the form, a woman dressed in red leather. "Who are you? What do you want?"

"Be wary of dragons, auntie. Especially red ones. They

aren't to be trusted. Bunch of big dumb liars." The woman pushed Zara into a black hole and the last thing she caught a glimpse of was a room filled with shiny Christmas ornaments.

The next second, she was on her hands and knees, ready to hurl. She swallowed and looked up. She was in the shadow of a great white wolf.

Her wolf.

HEAVY IS THE CROWN

*N*iko never wanted to be Wolf Tzar. That was for wolves far greater than he. Wolves who'd been groomed from birth to reign over their people with a firm but loving hand, sometimes a fist of steel. He realized he could and should be alpha of a pack, but that was as deep as his aspirations had gone.

One thing he knew to be true in this new and harsh world he found himself fighting for a place in, he would never let the likes of the Volkovs, or any other self-serving entities influence Wolfkind ever again. If that meant he had to sacrifice his own dream of living a peaceful life with his small pack, so be it.

Niko would die a hundred times every day searching for her. He would love her for a thousand years and never stop looking. He had to have faith that he would find her, that their hearts would beat for each other, their souls would reach for each other, until they could be together once again.

He would believe love would find a way. Because fate deigned they belonged to each other. Forever.

Dumuzid, and whoever he worked for, had awakened not only Niko's sleeping beast, but that of the wolves of the world. There was no way he was smart enough to concoct a conspiracy this deep on his own, much less done all the subterfuge to carry it out for a century or more. Rasputin was a powerful figure in their community, but he was only one wolf.

This went deeper than a corrupt ruling body.

Mikhail must have known and had died fighting against these dark forces. Niko would fight his name in every battle as a badge of honor just for having fought by a great wolf's side. A wolf who should have been Tzar for many years to come.

Now Niko had to fill his considerable paw prints.

He stood over the slashed body of Rasputin and resolved to pledge each second of his life to finding his mate and ending this tyranny dead in its tracks.

Wolves of Serenity Bay, I have claimed you as my own, though I would have deferred to your pack's heir if she wanted to step up. I ask you now to follow me into battle against an unknown foe who seeks to terrorize our very livelihood. They have controlled and shaped our culture from the inside, twisting our ideals until we no longer recognize the difference between right and wrong.

Wolves all around the circle lifted their voices to the darkened sky in support. Including his brothers and their mates. He had no right to ask them to risk their packs and the peace they'd been able to find, but he would beg their favor anyway.

Family, do you join me? Can you pledge the Troika, Grimm, and Bay packs to the cause, help me search for my mate, and take out the evil trying to ruin the wolf's way of life?

Max's great big black animal towered over all the other

wolves gathered in the sacred circle, except for Kosta's grey wolf, and of course Niko's own white one. Max stepped into the sacred space, followed by Galyna in her pretty brown wolf form. The two of them walked right up to Niko, Max's face level with his brother's. His blue eyes glowed bright and he stared into Niko's gaze as if he could see all of his intentions.

The black wolf took one step back, bent his leg, and bowed his head. *I, Maxsim Piotryvich Troika, alpha of the Troika pack, pledge our fealty to you, Nikolai Piotryvich Troika, Tzar of the Wolves.*

Niko's chest expanded with the love, loyalty, and gratitude pounding through his heart for his brother. The one who'd also never thought to be an alpha and who had stepped up in Niko's stead.

Thank you, brother.

Galyna bent her leg and bowed her head. *I, Galyna Shirvan, alpha of the Grimm pack, pledge our fealty to you, Tzar of the Wolves.*

Such a bold and brave woman his brother had been fated to mate. *Thank you, sister.*

Kosta sauntered up, scratched a few leaves out of his way, winked at Niko and bent his leg and bowed. *I, Konstantin Piotryvich Troika, alpha of the Bay pack, along with my mate Helinka, vow our loyalty to you, Wolf Tzar.*

Heli's beautiful golden wolf kicked the leaves back toward her mate, bowed and licked her chops. *What he said. Especially if I get to cater the coronation party. Then let's kick some demon butt.*

Niko stifled his laugh. Again, a beautiful brave woman, and this one with more than enough sass for his brother, had been fated by the Goddess for a lifetime of love. That all wolves would be so lucky. *Thank you, little sister.*

Who you calling little? Heli walked back to the edge of the circle wagging her tail, Kosta right behind her. Gal followed, but Max stayed another moment.

Make your claim, Nikolai.

Niko tipped his head to the side, confused. *I have.*

No, you claimed the Crescents, now Serenity Bay. You have yet to claim all of your wolves. They need to hear you ascend to your rightful place and take all of wolfkind into your stead.

Niko took a long deep breath. Max was correct. It wasn't what Niko thought he deserved, but he would fulfill the responsibility because it was what was right. He nodded at Max and waited until his brother returned to the others. The wolves looking on went as still and silent as the moonless night.

Niko reared up, raising his head and forelegs to the sky and howled for all to hear. He landed again like a hammer. His alpha voice rang out into the night, not only to those in the vicinity, but into the minds of all.

Hear me wolfkind, hear me and raise your voices with mine if you would have me as your leader. I vow my life to each and every one of you, and I pledge my fealty to all of you. I swear to serve you as your True Alpha. I claim you all as my pack, as Tzar of the Wolves.

The Serenity Bay pack raised their cries in acceptance of him once again, but theirs weren't the only joining them. Howls from the next closest pack in Falmouth could be heard even from miles away. Then howls from Plymouth and Marshfield joined the chorus. Fall River, Plymouth, Narraganset, Nantucket, and more packs that were farther afield than should be able to hear blended their wolf song with the others.

Niko's mind, filled with the sound of wolves from all around the world, from one end of the Americas to the other, from Africa, to Australia, and all the way back to Mother Russia. They voiced their choice to be claimed by him, their choice to make him their new Wolf Tzar.

No more did a corrupt outdated ruling class decide their fates. They chose to have him as their leader.

Niko's heart filled with gratitude and determination. It would be overflowing, save the giant missing chunk that was his one piece of sunshine in this world, his *solnyshka*. He bowed his head and with all the might of his alpha of all alpha's voice, whispered her name.

Zarenity.

Come back to me.

The sky crackled with electricity, the ground shook, and wind whipped through the night air. The shadows cast by his own body from the small light of the stars grew around him...

...and then, she was there.

"Niko?" Zara lie face up in the grass and leaves underneath him, her face beneath his muzzle, her chest and heart pounding against his, her limbs stretched out under his legs.

He blinked. Twice. Was she really here? He stared down at her, willing her form to be real, to feel her skin against his fur.

"Hey, love of my life. You're drooling on me and while I like you a lot, that's kind of gross."

Niko shifted, this time without the popping of bones and slicing of his fur to make way for skin. He simply was a man. He was a beast. He was both.

The power inside that he hadn't figured out was his own

life force becoming whole. He'd never lost his wolf, he was the wolf. Now he understood.

Zara's hands touched his cheeks and she wiped away one solitary tear, then pulled his head down for a kiss. She tasted of moonlight, sunshine, salt and sugar, spices and cream. She was his everything and she made him even more than he could be on his own, not whole, but more than he was on his own. Together, they were better than he could ever be.

He swept his tongue through her mouth, thrusting in and out, dueling with her, winning his dominance over her lips once again with a groan of ecstasy. She shoved her hands into his hair and wrapped her knees around his hips. He could get lost in her body.

"Ahem."

Zara froze with her tongue halfway down his throat. She sank back, away from him. That wouldn't do. Niko swept his hands under her ass and pulled her tighter to his chest.

"Ah... Hem."

Zara broke their kiss and Niko growled at her.

"Sweetheart, while I'm thoroughly looking forward to what I feel nice and hard against my undies, maybe not with a hundred people and or wolves watching?"

Grr. "I will take you how and when I want. I will claim you as my mate as witnessed by my pack. You are mine."

"I love when you get all growly and possessive." She stroked his cheek. "But that is a corpse lying next to us. Also, you've got blood on you. If we're gonna do this. Let's do it right, not because we were both scared to death, we'd just lost each other. I'm here. You're here. Neither of us is dead."

More grr. "Fine, but once we are cleaned up, I'm fucking

you long and hard regardless of who is watching or where we are."

"I'm amenable to that, but I wouldn't mind if it was in a nice soft bed instead of the field. I think there are leaves trying to get into my butt." She kissed the tip of his nose.

"Nothing is allowed into your luscious ass except me." Wasn't that a delicious prospect?

"Promises, promises." She grinned at him and her eyes danced with lust. Fuck, he was a lucky wolf.

Niko took her mouth in a deep kiss again just for good measure and when she was whimpering, picked her up and into his arms in one move. "Pack. My mate has returned. Tonight is for celebration. Tomorrow we go to war with the darkness."

Wolves yipped and yowled, several shifted back into human forms, and a few grabbed each other into loving embraces. It had been ages since these people had been allowed to celebrate, and even longer since they'd chosen their own mates. "There's one more thing I have to do before we go get wet together."

"At the next full moon, we will have our first mating ceremony as the Serenity Pack. If you think you've been blessed with a true mate, or even hope that you have, invite them, whether they be wolf, human, or something in between. As my first proclamation as your Tzar, I declare that you are free to mate and love whomever you choose. Love is love and you deserve to have a mate who wants, craves, and needs you as much as I do my own heart's desire."

"You're such a romantic." Zara laid her head on his shoulder and sighed happily.

"I thought it was a slightly more appropriate speech than to tell them to go get into whoever's pants they could."

"Wait a minute. Did you just say that was your first proclamation as their Tzar? What did I miss?"

Niko laughed and walked toward the pack house. "Nothing much. Where did you go?"

"I—" She frowned, and her eyes flicked back and forth while she thought. "I'm not sure. Somewhere bad. But somebody helped me get back to you. I don't think I'm supposed to remember and I'm okay with that. My chest gets uncomfortable just thinking about it."

With his heart in his throat, pinching it almost closed, he prayed he'd never have to apologize like this to her ever again. "I'm sorry I couldn't save you from Dumuzid and that goddamned dragon. I hope things ended badly for him wherever you were."

"Nikolai Troika, you shush your face right now. We are a team and you don't have to take responsibility for something evil forces do. You're a good man and we will face whatever comes at us, and we won't be perfect, but we'll be together."

Niko kicked the front door open and carried her across the threshold of their new house, the place they would make into a home for each other, goddess willing, their children, and all of wolfkind. But for now, his mate wanted some privacy and a bed. The rest would come later.

As would she. Come over and over and over.

The days ahead would not always be easy. Not everyone in wolfkind would like that the mystical Volkov's weren't there to tell them how to think anymore. The one-bloods would push back, and he feared that not only would he and his brothers have to fight the darkness they had battled tonight, but perhaps some of their own as well.

Being allowed to live their lives and find true love would change the minds of many. He would do his best to be an example of how to treat a mate. Zara would not only be the matriarch of the Serenity Pack, but she would be the Tsarina of all wolfkind. A duty he had no doubt she would fulfill amazingly. She'd probably be a better guiding light than he would. Thank the Goddess she was here by his side.

But first he wanted her under him.

"Nikolai Piotryvich Troika. Where are you, young man?"

Niko froze and looked at Zara. Her eyes were wide, matching his expression exactly. "Is that your mom?"

"Yep. If we slip into the closest bedroom and pretend we didn't hear her can we–"

"No. I was always worried your parents didn't like me and I never understood why your dad got all wound up about us. I will not start off our life together on a bad note with your mother. Put me down."

Dog gone it. He set her down and yelled down the stairs. "We're up here, mom."

Selena Troika bounded up the stairway and pulled Zara into a big hug. "*Rypka*, welcome to the family. I'm here for tea and cookies."

Zara hugged his meddling parent back and mouthed a question to him. "What does *rypka* mean?"

Niko chuckled and made a fish-face at her. She wrinkled up her nose. His mother was so involved in giving all of her affection to Zara, this hugging business could go on for a while. "It's like honey or sweetheart, I swear."

"You're teaching me Russian."

That could be fun. "Only if I get to teach you all the naughty words first."

"Of course." She winked at him.

"Mom. I love you. Go make yourself at home. We will see you tomorrow."

Selena released Zara and smiled. She wasn't dumb and knew exactly what he was saying. She socked him in the arm. "*Umnitza*. I'm very proud of you. Go on now. I'll get to planning your coronation and the mating ritual."

She rubbed her hands together and walked away examining the decor as she went. "Oh, we're replacing that, and that. How garish. Who were these people? There are other ways to decorate a pack house other than paintings of wolves and the moon."

"Mother."

"I'm going, I'm going. Don't wear each other out too much." She waved at them over her shoulder and descended the stairs. "On second thought, do. It'll keep you out of my hair. I can't believe all my boys have found their mates. Finally."

Niko shook his head and then picked Zara back up like the princess, or rather Tsarina, she was. She giggled. "That will never get old."

"Good, because I'll never tire of carrying you off to my bed.

HOWLING AT THE MOON

*T*he second night of the full moon bloomed calm and clear. Tonight was her mating ritual, where she and Niko would be officially wolf-married. Selena, Heli, and Galyna had all helped her prepare. Not only would she become Niko's mate in the eyes of the combined packs of Serenity Bay, the Troikas, the Grimms, and the Bay pack, she was also to be crowned Tsarina of the Wolves.

It had taken a lot of hard work and practice, but she was ready for the evening and her surprise for Niko was all set. Mostly. Probably.

The packs were already gathered, and Niko waited in the sacred circle for her. She walked barefoot through the woods in the lightweight white shift she'd borrowed from Galyna, aware of every wolf that ran in the trees around her. The Enforcers were there to protect her on her short journey from the pack house to the ceremony, but she stepped confidently. She'd seen everything in a vision just this morning.

She hadn't let her second sight go too far, she didn't want to spoil all the fun she and Niko were going to get up to, but she had seen that the night would go off without a hitch. Whoever or whatever had been tormenting wolfkind was, for lack of another word, busy.

Niko had vowed to continue to search for any threat to his people, but he also wanted peace for them all, especially since he feared battles on the home-front were ahead.

Zara tried to assuage the worst of his stresses by searching their futures. She had better control of her gift now. She could close her eyes and see snippets of events to come. Most easily if she had a specific thing she was looking for. Although, sometimes she was still surprised with an unexpected vision. Those weren't as common anymore. Not since she'd truly accepted her ability and how she could use it to serve those around her.

She and Niko had worked tirelessly the past few weeks to return all those who had been trafficked back to their homes, or to facilities that could support them through dealing with the trauma. Some had chosen to stay, and a few would be at tonight's mating ritual. In fact, there were quite a few human women here tonight.

Galyna and Heli had helped create a welcoming environment for all the interspecies couples. More wolves had sought out their true mates under Ramsey Crescent's rule than he would have liked. Good for them. Ramsey could rot in hell with... hmm. Once again, she couldn't grasp onto a thought that should have come easily.

Wolfkind was still getting used to the idea that they were allowed to find true mates and Selena had become quite the matchmaker. She was even thinking of starting a wolf shifter matchmaking agency. Turned out, she had a special gift of her own. Selena Troika could see fated mates glow for each other.

Zara could hardly wait for what that looked like for herself.

She twisted the brand-new necklace her parents had sent from their work campaigning to save the endangered snow leopards in Russia. The necklace was a miniature Faberge egg and had a charm on a little chain inside. The note indicated the charm was quite old, according to the peasant woman they'd bought it from.

The surprise had come out of nowhere, but the card accompanying it from her mom said she'd seen that Zara needed a special gift. The word seen had been in quotes.

She would be asking her mother about that when they returned from their trip...in five months.

The clearing containing the Serenity Pack's sacred circle was another ten yards ahead of her. She paused for just a moment and picked a flower in her path with pretty little blue flowers and placed it in her hair. Now she was ready.

Zara stepped from the shadows into the light of the moon and walked toward the man of her dreams. Niko was so handsome, standing naked as the day he was born, he took her breath away. His eyes glowed with the amber color she'd come to love that meant the wolf part of him was near the surface.

Tonight, it wasn't only his eyes that glowed. His entire body shimmered in the moonlight like he was some sort of an angel. He reached his hand out to her with the most breathtaking smile on his face, especially for her. "Zara, *solnyshka*, you're glowing. I've never seen anything so beautiful in my life."

"It must be because I'm so happy."

"I hope so. I intend to make you happy for as many days as

I possibly can, for the rest of our lives." He kissed her, slipping his tongue softly across her lips. "Are you ready?"

"I was born ready." She took a deep breath and lifted the dress over her head. She dropped it to the ground and then knelt before Niko. When she had her position settled, she looked up at him and the lust in his eyes sent the birds and the bees flurrying through her body in anticipation of what that look meant.

He cupped her chin in his hand and lifted her face. "Zarenity Alexandra Serdtse, do you acknowledge me as your true mate?"

"I do."

Niko rubbed his thumb across her bottom lip. "And do you submit to my rule as your Tzar."

"I do, as do all those gathered. We all kneel to you and pledge ourselves to your rule." As she said the words, all the people gathered around the sacred circle, knelt and bowed their heads.

Niko was supposed to tell them all to rise and celebrate their new Tsarina and to find their mates, but he stared down into her eyes for so long Zara was sure she was going to get lost in his gaze. It was filled with so much more than lust. In one simple look, he made her feel special, made her feel loved.

Quietly, for her ears only he asked her another question. "And do you, Zara, beat of my heart, submit to me, as the one who will always keep you, your pleasure, and your love sacred?"

Her heart could burst from the rush of emotions his words, his promise to her, warmed her from the inside out. "Oh, Niko... I do... You know I do."

He smiled and licked his lips. Then loud for all to hear he

declared, "Then I take you as my mate, and my Tsarina. Wolves, rise and celebrate love and life with me and the ones who holds my soul."

The howls could be heard for miles around, some human voices, some wolves, and many somewhere in between. After a moment, Niko raised his hand and quieted the crowd. "I wish for you all a true fated mate. If that person is here tonight, join us in the mating ritual. If not, may you find them soon and experience the joy I know."

Dozens of people moved into the sacred circle and found their someone special. Niko sank to his knees and pulled Zara in for their first kiss as true mates. "I love you, *solnyshka.*"

"I love you, *luibimyj.*" Zara had practiced the Russian term of endearment for true love for days on end. She hoped she said it right.

Niko grinned like she was the cutest thing he'd ever seen. "You are full of surprises, aren't you?"

"There's more where that came from." She hadn't even revealed her big surprise yet.

"Come here." Niko wrapped his arms around her and they quickly snaked her down to her butt. "I do love this ass of yours."

He'd made that abundantly clear the past few weeks. He was even a little obsessed with her butt. Not that she minded his attentions. She would need to invest in a lingerie company with how many pairs of panties he'd ripped off of her. Either that or stop wearing them at all.

Niko noticed her grin. Not like she was trying to hide it. He slid his fingers across her ass. "Do you want me to take you here tonight, in front of all the other lovers? Will you let me possess you like that for all to see how your body is mine."

Giddy butterflies flittered from her stomach and dropped between her legs. "You're the one in charge."

"I do love how kinky you are, my mate. Turn around, on your hands and knees, ass in the air. But I want your eyes up. I want you to see how your beauty and submission turns everyone else on, how you are craved by all, but belong only to me."

Zara felt beautiful when she was with Niko, but she hadn't enjoyed that same confidence in her own body or her own sexuality in society's eyes before him. With Niko behind her, ready to possess her body, she was more than beautiful. She was sex incarnate.

The sounds of other people coupling around them only sent her own desire skyrocketing.

"Open yourself for me." Niko spread her legs and teased her entrance with the head of his cock. She spread her legs wider and prayed that he wouldn't tease them both for long. He slid his fingers in, testing to see if she was ready.

"Wet for me already? Such a good girl." He pushed his cock into her pussy in one slow and agonizing long, deep thrust. "Fuck, your cunt feels so good, Zara. I will never get enough of you."

He withdrew and drove into her again, just as slow, driving them both mad with need. He could do this for hours, making her wait to come until she was crazy with desire. She knew better than to beg. Yet.

"That's it, love." Niko leaned over her body and grabbed one of her arms. He waited for her to readjust her weight, so they didn't both go tumbling over. Then he guided her hand between her legs. "Put your fingers in your pretty, wet pussy.

Stroke your clit for me. But don't you dare come until I tell you to... Got it?"

"Yes." Her voice was already husky, and more breath than sound.

Niko started her fingers swirling over her sensitive clit and when he was satisfied she was doing as he asked, he grabbed a hold of her hips and fucked her in earnest, driving in and out of her hard and fast. She wouldn't be able to hold back this orgasm, not tonight. She loved when he made her wait, driving her higher into extasy than she thought she could go. But this time, her body wasn't having it. Every synced movement between the two of them pushed her closer and closer to climax.

"Yes, Zara, Goddess, your cunt is squeezing me so tight. I'm not going to last much longer, your body is just too enticing." Ever in control, Niko slowed his thrusts and slid one of his hands between them to where their bodies met. He pushed two fingers into her pussy along with his cock, and drew her body's juices from her.

He pressed his wet fingers against her tight asshole and swirled them around and around, until she was high on his teasing touch and ready to beg him to push them in. But Niko knew her body and what she needed more than she did. First, he inserted one finger and then the other, scissoring them until she was so hot and panting that she could do nothing but moan. He'd pushed her beyond words and into incoherent pleas.

He pulled his fingers from her enticing torture, but quickly replaced them with his cock. "Take me, Zara. Take all of me."

He'd prepared her body, but he was so big that he took his

time pushing into her ass. "Rub your clit fast and hard, Zara. I'm going to come in about two thrusts and I want you coming with me."

She'd love to see and feel him lose control, but she doubted that was tonight. This taking of her body, taking her control and making it his own was his claim on her just as much as his mark.

He tortured her with the temptation of release as he pistoned in and out of her tight hole a dozen times before he lost his rhythm and shoved deep. She could hardly breathe with her need to come for him.

"Now, Zara, come for me now." He pulsed inside of her, marking her with his seed. "Fuck. I love you so much."

Together, their bodies shattered, taking them both spiraling into a nirvana they could only give to each other. Stars burst behind her eyes and Zara's vision tunneled as her body came so hard, every muscle locked and then fell crashing into pulsing bliss. The only thing she was aware of was the words of love pouring from Niko's mouth to her ear right before he sank his teeth into the mark on her shoulder, sending her skyrocketing into another orgasm.

They collapsed into the grass and Niko somehow had the wherewithal to pull her body over his own so that she didn't have to lay in the dirt. They curled together, chest to chest, feeling only the beating of their hearts for a long euphoric, dreamy time.

Niko was the first to recover some semblance of himself. "Christ, woman. You are going to kill me. How is it possible that every time we have sex, it gets better?"

"Mmm-hmm." She didn't have words for how he made her feel.

"You're so adorable when you're drunk on my love." He wrapped a hand into her hair and kissed the top of her head.

"I'll gladly stay intoxicated on you for a lifetime. I love you, Niko."

"I love you more than ever. Every time I see you, or think of you, or smell you, I love you more than the second before."

Zara giggled. "Smell me?"

He petted her hair and said, "It's a wolf thing."

"Is it? I'd like to experience that for myself."

"You seem to be the one person in the pack I can't use my alpha voice on and compel to shift." He didn't sound that bothered, but she knew he'd love it if he could see her as a wolf too.

"Are you sure about that?" This was going to be fun.

"Zara, my mate," the alpha voice rang out like electricity, "shift. Bring the wolf inside of you out for all to see." While he said the words, she could tell he didn't believe it would do anything, just by the way he continued to hold her in his arms.

But with a little bit of concentration on her end, he held a furry wolf instead of the woman. Niko sat bolt upright and stared at her dumbfounded. So, she licked his face. *Are you going to sit there all night, my Tzar, or are you going to go on a run with me?*

In a flash, Niko's huge white wolf stood next to her and he licked her nose, which was fair. *You are the most gorgeous wolf, I've ever seen. Come, my love, run through the woods, hunt with me, and howl at the moon.*

Niko took off across the sacred circle and after a couple of faulty steps, Zara found her feet, got them coordinated and ran after him. She howled and was surprised how much fun that was, so she did it again.

Niko joined his voice with hers and even without words, she knew he was telling the Moon Goddess above how much he loved her.

Wolves from near and far howled at the moon, into the clear night sky. This was a new age for their kind. One that had battles ahead, but that would also be filled with love and happiness because the days of selfish leaders was over. Together she and Niko would show the world exactly how to live happily ever after.

———

NEED MORE NIKO AND ZARA? I've got a bonus epilogue and deleted scenes for you!

Join my Curvy Connection and I'll send it to you right away!

Join here —> http://geni.us/MoreKinkyWolf

If you're already a member, check your email!

WANT to read more about the Troika Wolf Pack?

—> Check out the Dragons Love Curves series because their fates are all intertwined and the Troika boys and their mates make special guest appearances all throughout the series! Turn the page for an excerpt from the first book in the series - Chase Me

A TASTE OF HUNGRY WOLF

Naughty Ladies

Helena surveyed her new office in the back of the Naughty Wolf and pinched herself just to make sure it was all real.

Ouch.

Yep. She wasn't dreaming and she was going to have a bruise on the back of her hand. That was okay. It wasn't like the kind of guys who came to a gentlemen's club were looking at her hands. She'd take that mark all day, every day, twice on Sundays, if it meant this new life she'd built was real.

Kosta had given her this big fat promotion and it was exactly the break she needed. Sure, she made good money dancing. Despite what society and her ex might think, her plus-size ass was in high demand for lap dances among the gentleman who frequented the club. But getting promoted to manager meant she had a whole lot more job stability. She got a cut of the whole club's take each night and that meant she'd finally be able to pay off the mountain of debt her jackass ex had left her with.

A gaggle of giggles sounded from the hallway, breaking the silence of the empty club. Helena frowned. She'd come in early for her first day as manager and hadn't expected any of the girls to come in for hours.

"Helena, we brought champagne to celebrate your promotion." Daphine, Debbie Joy, Heather, Kerrie, and Michelle stuck their heads in through the office door. Daphine held an inexpensive bottle in the air and Michelle waved some plastic flutes at her.

Despite her best efforts to be all business, her mouth turned up in a warm smile at them. The other dancers at the club were the closest she had to friends besides Heli. "Come on in, girly-girls, and pour me a glass. I should have known you wouldn't let me actually get any work done."

"Really? Awesome." The five ladies looked at each other like they were surprised Helena was down for celebrating. They half-fell into the room and plunked down on any available flat surface.

The champagne cork popped, and the wine and gossip flowed. "Of course we're not going to let you work. You already work too hard."

Helena took her glass of bubbles and took a sip to appease the girls. "Yeah, keeping your butts out of trouble."

Debbie Joy turned her yoga-pants-clad butt cheek toward Helena and slapped it. "No, that's what the bouncers are for. Has anyone else noticed how every single dude Kosta gets to work here is, like, ultra good-looking?"

Everyone nodded. Heather sighed and looked all dreamy. "Yeah…and built."

"Not to mention hung like an elephant." Kerrie waggled her eyebrows.

Michelle faux gasped. "Wait. How do you know that? Oooh. Are you sleeping with a bouncer?"

Helena let the girls have their fun for a few more minutes. She'd shoo them away in a bit so she could dig into the mountain of paperwork Kosta had left her. He was giving her a whole hell of a lot of responsibility and she intended to earn her keep. Neither Kosta nor Heli were around as much anymore since they'd taken on the project of restoring the Inn at the Bay.

Out of all the employees of the Naughty Wolf, she alone knew the real reason her boss and best friend spent all their time down at the Bay. These ladies with all their giggles and gossip had no idea the bouncers were all actually something more than well-built, sexy, hot tough guys.

So much more.

If she hadn't seen Kosta turn into a wolf with her own eyes, she probably still wouldn't believe it. Since that day it was so obvious to her which men in their little town had the beast inside of them, and which didn't. The wolf pack guys had this innate confidence, an easy and relaxed swagger that she found a little too enticing.

Which was a bad thing. She was not going there. Not with any man or wolf. She was perfectly fine on her own, thank you very much.

Daphine topped off everyone's glasses. "So, Helena. Now that you're in charge, we have a favor to ask."

Uh-oh. Helena looked around the circle at the hopeful, expectant faces. Crap. What did they want from her?

Michelle snort-laughed. "Don't look at us like we're going

to ask you for your first-born child. We just want to know if you would host Thanksgiving here this year. None of us has family around."

"Or if we do, we aren't spending an entire freaking day with them." Heather rolled her eyes and then her head, like spending time with her family induced a demonic possession or at least a painful kink in the neck.

Kerrie shrugged. "We want to spend it with the people here, they're the family we choose, you know?"

Ah. Helena did know. While she did her best to keep men at arm's length, the women at the club were more important to her than any imagined mom or sisters she'd never had, and getting kicked out of the house at seventeen didn't exactly make her feel warm and fuzzy toward her puritanical father. Holidays were never very big in their house.

"You didn't have to bribe me with champagne to ask that. I'm happy for all of us to have Thanksgiving dinner here. I'll even bring the pie." It would be nice to share a meal and talk about what they were grateful for.

"And a date," Debbie Joy said, folding her arms.

Not this again. They were eternally on her to find a man. "What? No. That would be one more person to split the pie with."

Suddenly all eyes were on her like she'd just fallen flat on her face on stage. Kerrie folder her arm and slumped into an exaggerated pout. "We never get to meet your boyfriends."

"That's because she doesn't have any," Daphine jibed.

Kerrie, who was newer to their made-up little family, grimaced. "Oops. Sorry. We'd like to meet your girlfriend."

Daphine gave Kerrie a shove. "That's not what I meant."

Another woman stuck her head in the office. "What's this I hear about a Thanksgiving dinner?"

"Selena, hi. We were just talking about having dinner here for the employees after we close on Thursday. You don't think Kosta will mind, will he?"

"Well, I just love the idea. I was on my way here to see if anyone wanted to come up to my house, but this sounds like a whole lot more fun. You don't mind if I crash, do you?"

What, like they were going to say no to the owner's mother? "Of course you can come too."

"Oh goodie. I'll tell the boys we're having dinner here. Shall we do potluck style? I have just the man to set you up with for dinner, Helena. You're going to simply love him. I already have several heritage turkeys thawing in the fridge. Lots of meat eaters in my family, you know. I'm sure Heli is going to want to go overboard on pies. Mmm. Pie. I'll just set up a quick Google Doc for everyone to sign up to say what they're bringing. I'll email you all in a few minutes. I can't wait to meet your young gentlemen, ladies. See you all on Thursday." Selena walked back out of the office, tapping away on her phone screen.

Mouths hung open, eyes stared wide, and the five of them waited silently for a full minute until they heard the back door open and then close. Debbie Joy was the first one to regain her mouth to brain coordination. "Wait. What just happened? Did we just get steamrolled into having Thanksgiving dinner with the Troikas?"

"Yep." Helena took a big gulp of her champagne.

Heather automatically refilled the glass. "And did she say she's setting you up on a blind date?"

Sigh. Helena drained every last dribble of the bubbles. "I was hoping I'd imagined that."

Crap. Helena did not need a date. How the hell was she going to get out of this one?

She'd just have to develop a case of the clumsies and spill her pie all over his pants before dinner even started. No, pie was too precious, especially if it came from The Sleepy Folk's pie shop. Gravy. Yeah, perfect. Brown gravy from sternum to crotch would send any unwanted date running.

It would be so much better if she could figure out a way to get out of the date in the first place, though, so the poor slob Selena wanted to set her up with didn't have to suffer a mashed potato and gravy fate.

Hmm. Did she feel a sore throat coming on?

No. No she did not. Ugh. Even if she did, Selena and the girls would probably come drag her out of bed, pretty her up, and drag her butt to the dinner anyway.

Oh, oh, oh. What if they didn't close the club that night and the dinner had to be hosted somewhere else? No, the Naughty Wolf was never open on holidays. Kosta insisted the staff have time off and even usually gave them all bonuses. He wouldn't keep it open just because Helena told him to, even if she was his new manager.

Fine. She was back to the gravy plan. She'd sign up to provide very hot, like boiling, gravy for the dinner and spill it right on any guy she didn't recognize who walked through the door on Thursday evening.

"Helena," Daphine's tone was much too close to parental. "What are you plotting?"

"Nothing. Only thinking about what dish to bring." Which was one-hundred percent true.

"I think we'd better relegate you to rolls, otherwise you're liable to spill a perfectly good green bean casserole on some poor unsuspecting schmoe."

"I would never..." She was so busted, and totally screwed.

Not even in the fun way. Not that she even remembered what that felt like.

Whatever. She had a couple of days to figure out how to get out of this blind date. No way was she going to let her Friendsgiving be ruined by a random dude.

ALSO BY AIDY AWARD

Alpha Wolves Want Curves

Dirty Wolf

Naughty Wolf

Kinky Wolf

Hungry Wolf

The Fate of the Wolf Guard

Unclaimed

Untamed

Undone

Undefeated

Dragons Love Curves

Chase Me

Tease Me

Unmask Me

Bite Me

Cage Me

Baby Me

Defy Me

Surprise Me

Dirty Dragon

Crave Me

Slay Me

The Black Dragon Brotherhood

Tamed

Tangled

Twisted

Fated For Curves

A Touch of Fate

A Tangled Fate

A Twist of Fate

The Curvy Love Series

Curvy Diversion

Curvy Temptation

Curvy Persuasion

The Curvy Seduction Saga

Rebound

Rebellion

Reignite

Rejoice

Revel

By Aidy Award and Piper Fox

Big Wolf on Campus

Cocky Jock Wolf

Bad Boy Wolf

Heart Throb Wolf

ABOUT THE AUTHOR

Aidy Award is a curvy girl who kind of has a thing for stormtroopers. She's also the author of the popular Curvy Love series and the hot new Dragons Love Curves series. She writes curvy girl erotic romance, about real love, and dirty fun, with happy ever afters because every woman deserves great sex and even better romance, no matter her size, shape, or what the scale says.

Read the delicious tales of hot heroes and curvy heroines come to life under the covers and between the pages of Aidy's books. Then let her know because she really does want to hear from her readers.

Connect with Aidy on her website. www.AidyAward.com get her Curvy Connection, and join her Facebook Group - Aidy's Amazeballs.